D0178043

14 JUL 2014 CD
-9 SEP 2014 CD
22 SEP 2014 CD
-3 NOV 2014 CD
-7 NOV 2014 CD
11 APR 2016
JUN 2016
06 JUL 2017
WITHDRAWN
DUMFRIES AND GALLOWAY LIBRARIES

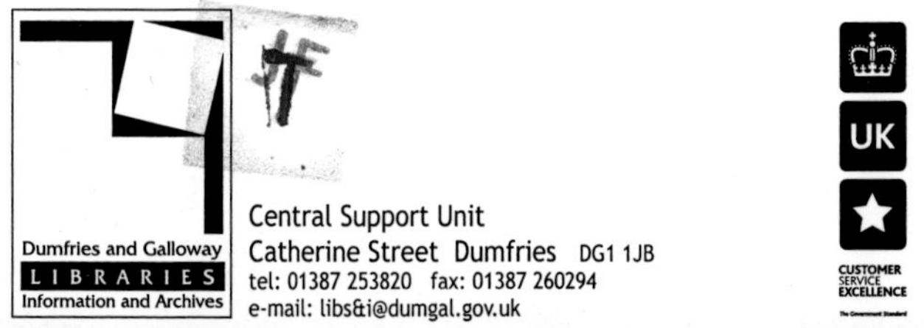
Dumfries and Galloway
LIBRARIES
Information and Archives
UK
CUSTOMER SERVICE EXCELLENCE

THE NEW PATROL

Titles by Andy McNab:

The New Recruit

DROPZONE

Dropzone

Dropzone: Terminal Velocity

BOY SOLDIER (with Robert Rigby)

Boy Soldier

Payback

Avenger

Meltdown

For adults:

Bravo Two Zero

Immediate Action

Seven Troop

Spoken from the Front

Novels:

Aggressor

Battle Lines (with Kym Jordan)

Brute Force

Crisis Four

Crossfire

Dark Winter

Dead Centre

Deep Black

Exit Wound

Firewall

Last Light

Liberation Day

Recoil

Red Notice

Remote Control

Silencer

War Torn (with Kym Jordan)

Zero Hour

ANDY McNAB

THE NEW PATROL

DOUBLEDAY

THE NEW PATROL
A DOUBLEDAY BOOK
Hardback: 978 0 857 53332 6
Trade Paperback: 978 0 857 53333 3

Published in Great Britain by Doubleday,
an imprint of Random House Children's Publishers UK
A Random House Group Company

This edition published 2014

1 3 5 7 9 10 8 6 4 2

With thanks to David Gatward

The Random House Group Limited supports the Forest Stewardship Council® (FSC®), the leading international forest-certification organisation. Our books carrying the FSC label are printed on FSC®-certified paper. FSC is the only forest-certification scheme supported by the leading environmental organisations, including Greenpeace. Our paper procurement policy can be found at www.randomhouse.co.uk/environment

Set in Adobe Garamond

RANDOM HOUSE CHILDREN'S PUBLISHERS UK
61–63 Uxbridge Road, London W5 5SA

Addresses for comp… be found at:

THE R…

A CIP catalo… brary.

Pri…

ARMY RANKS

OFFICER RANKS	
RANK	RESPONSIBILITIES
Officer Cadet	Trainee Officer rank
Second Lieutenant	Lead up to 30 soldiers
Lieutenant	Lead up to 30 soldiers. Increased responsibilities
Captain	Typically second-in-command of a sub-unit of up to 120 soldiers
Major	Lead up to 120 soldiers and officers. Training and welfare management
Lieutenant Colonel	Unit commander (up to 650 soldiers and officers). Ensure overall operational effectiveness of their unit
Colonel	Typically serve as staff officers between field commands
Brigadier	Brigade commander (up to 5,000 soldiers and officers)
Major General	Division commander (up to 15,000 soldiers and officers)
Lieutenant General	Senior Army Officer
General	Senior Army Officer

OTHER RANKS	
RANK	RESPONSIBILITIES
Private	First rank
Lance Corporal	Supervise 3–4 soldiers
Corporal	Supervise 7–8 soldiers
Sergeant	Second-in-command of a troop of up to 35 soldiers
Staff/Colour Sergeant	Man and resource management of up to 120 soldiers
Warrant Officer Class 2 (Company/ Squadron Sergeant Major)	Senior management role, focusing on training, welfare and discipline of up to 120 personnel
Warrant Officer Class 1 (Regimental Sergeant Major)	Most senior soldier rank. Senior adviser to Unit commander with leadership, welfare and discipline responsibility of up to 650 personnel

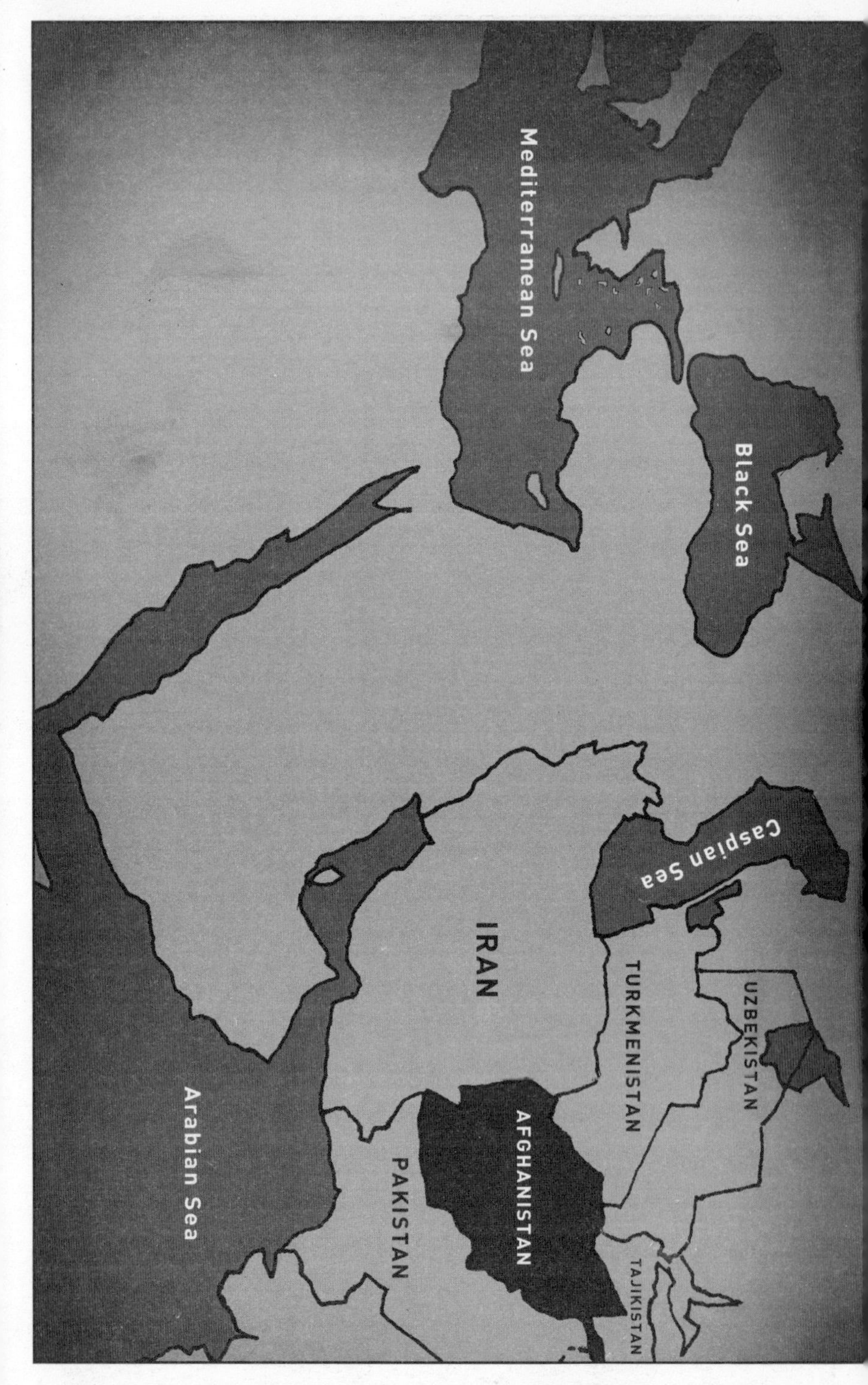

These maps show the approximate location of Afghanistan and Helmand Province in relation to the surrounding areas.

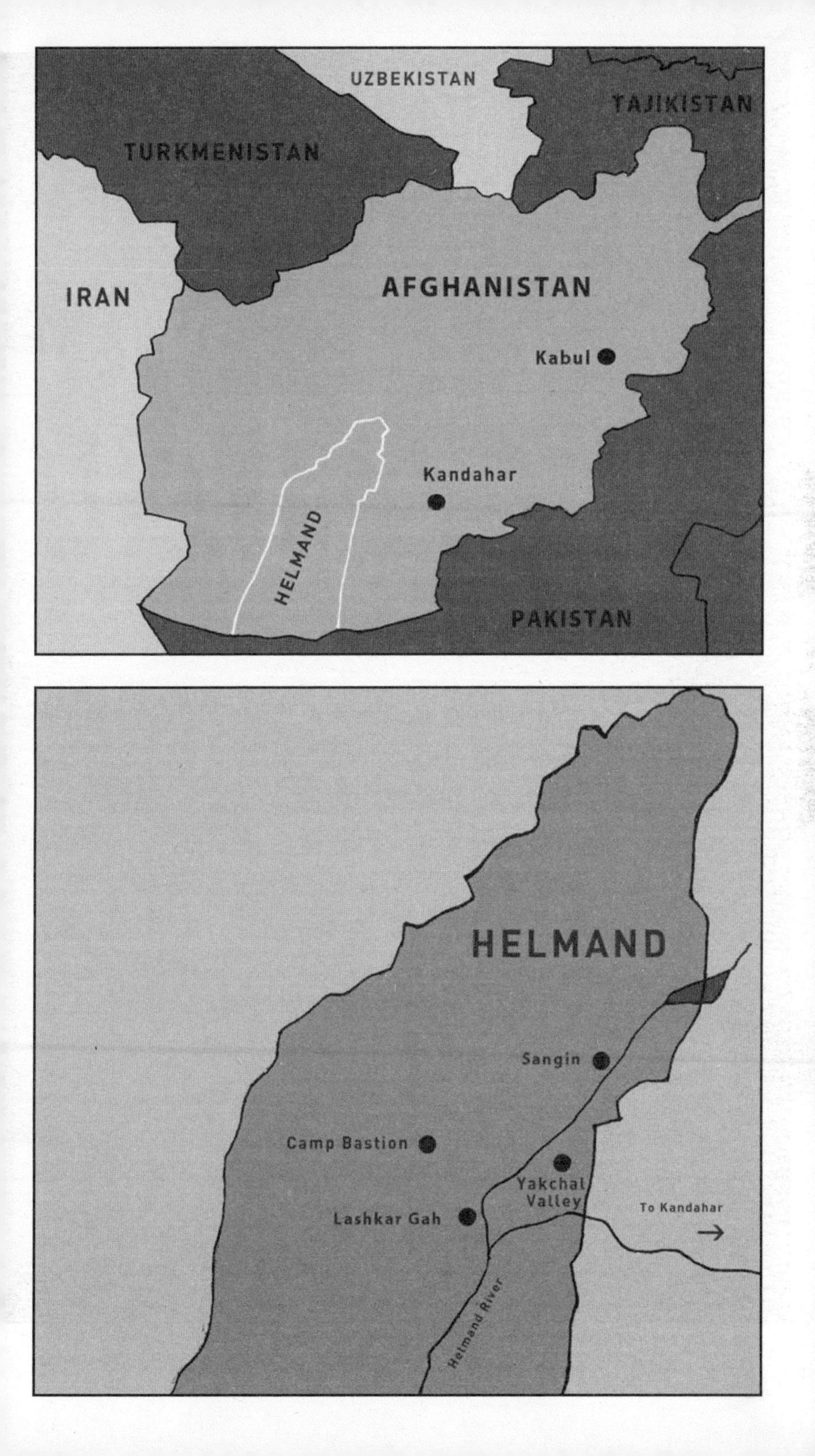
UZBEKISTAN
TAJIKISTAN
TURKMENISTAN
IRAN
AFGHANISTAN
Kabul
Kandahar
HELMAND
PAKISTAN
HELMAND
Sangin
Camp Bastion
Yakchal
Valley
Lashkar Gah
To Kandahar
Helmand River

Glossary

ACOG – Advanced Combat Optical Gunsight providing up to 6x fixed power magnification, illuminated at night by an internal phosphor

ANA – Afghan National Army

bayonet – a knife designed to fit in, on, over or underneath the muzzle of a rifle

camel bak – a large water reservoir that can be carried in a soldier's backpack

Camp Bastion – a fortified base for the Coalition Forces in the Helmand Province of Afghanistan

Card Alpha – a yellow laminated card carried by every British soldier setting out the strict Rules of Engagement of the British Army

Catterick – one of the British Army's main training camps

Chinook – helicopter, most often used for transporting equipment or troops; known by soldiers as 'cows'

GLOSSARY

C17 – a large military aircraft used to transport troops and equipment

contact – any action involving the enemy and the discharge of weapons

Dari – one of the two official languages spoken in Afghanistan

FOB – Forward Operating Base

Foxhound – a patrol vehicle specifically designed and built to protect against the threats faced by troops in Afghanistan

GPMG – General-Purpose Machine Gun, nicknamed the 'Gimpy'; belt-driven

ground sight – a term used for keeping a keen eye on the ground ahead for anything unusual

Hellfires – missiles predominantly fired by Apache

HESCO – multi-cellular wall units, filled with whatever material is available to hand, such as sand, and used to protect patrol bases. Tested against charges of up to 20,000lb

IED – an Improvised Explosive Device, which can be placed on the ground or used by suicide bombers; sometimes activated by remote control

Infantry – the British Infantry is based on the tried and tested regimental system, which has proved successful on operations over the years; it consists of a number of regular and reserve battalions. The

British Infantry has a strong tradition of courage in battle

ISAF – International Security Assistance Force

JDAM – unguided gravity bomb; can have a guidance system bolted on so that it can be guided to a target by GPS

LASM – Light Anti-Structures Missile; a rocket launcher designed to be discarded after launch

medevac – emergency evacuation of a casualty from a war zone

multiple – group of soldiers numbering approximately 8–12 men

NCO – Non-Commissioned Officer, like a corporal or sergeant

padre – army chaplain

Pashto – one of the two official languages spoken in Afghanistan

PRR – Personal Role Radio: small transmitter-receiver radio that enables soldiers to communicate over short distances, and through buildings and walls

RODET – Roll Over Drill and Egress Training; to practise escape techniques from a rolled-over vehicle

RPG – Rocket-Propelled Grenade

RSOI – Reception, Staging, and Onward Integration: a process of acclimatization for troops newly out in Afghanistan

Rules of Engagement – strict rules laid out by armed forces worldwide on the use of lethal force

SA80 – semi-automatic rifle made by Heckler & Koch: the standard British Army rifle

sangar – sentry post

Sharpshooter – a highly accurate rifle, taking a 7.62 round, able to hit a target at up to 800 metres

SUSAT sight – this gives a 4x magnification and has tritium-powered illumination, thus allowing a soldier to carry on fighting when the light is low at dusk and dawn

TA – Territorial Army; volunteers who also hold down civilian jobs

Taliban – insurgents/tribal groups fighting for power in Afghanistan, nicknamed 'Terry' and 'Tally' by the Army

theatre – field of operations within a war

tour – period of active service; a normal tour in Afghanistan would be approximately six months

TRiM – Trauma Risk Management: a programme to ensure combatants have support after a traumatic incident, a sort of psychological first aid

UGL – under-slung grenade launcher, fitted to SA80

Wolfhound – a heavily armoured six-wheeled troop carrier

Prologue

With the sound of the patrol in the distance moving away, the figure slipped from cover and walked over to the trail. He had heard them approach, watched each soldier pass, not more than a few metres away from where he'd been hiding, wondered which one would fall victim to the device already hidden beneath the path. It didn't matter, though he had a particular distaste for the Afghans who had walked past in their western combat clothing, carrying American M16s. All he cared about was that one of them would step on it and that would be that, another dead enemy soldier.

Crouching down, the man checked the area carefully. He smiled. He liked this way of working, laying the IEDs in advance, then connecting them later to a battery once the enemy had been seen in the area. It meant that they – he and his Taliban brothers – could almost be sure of a kill.

Remembering where the device was laid, the man eventually found the connecting wires, pulling them up from beneath the rock that had hidden them. Then the battery was quickly attached and hidden once again. The whole task had taken less than a minute. He would be at a safe distance before the patrol headed back this way, and without any possibility of his tracks being discovered.

Carefully making his way back across the rough ground, the figure eventually came to a stop, dropping down behind a thick area of scrub, hidden in shadow under a collection of boulders.

The sun slipped further on its arc towards the end of the day. The man heard the sound of the patrol coming back. In a few moments there would be one less enemy to worry about. A cold, grim smile spread across his face . . .

1

'Get this down your neck, Scott, you pasty-faced bastard!'

Liam Scott, eighteen years old, just back from his first tour in Afghanistan, had barely recovered from the night before. He turned towards Jason Finch, a Geordie born and bred, who was holding what looked like the devil's own drink – a glass filled with something thick and blood red. Unsteady on his feet, Liam grabbed the glass-topped counter. The bar girl backed away, clearly concerned that whatever was in his stomach was about to go rapidly mobile.

'My arm hurts,' he said.

He hadn't bothered to get changed, just had the shower-in-a-can courtesy of a hefty all-over blast of body spray.

'What did you expect?' said Jason, standing at the bar

like it had been built just for him. 'Tattoos don't usually tickle.'

Liam snapped round. 'What?'

Jason reached over and rolled up the sleeve of Liam's right arm. Under a large patch of cling film, stuck to the arm with tape, was a greasy mess of white and pink covering a tattoo.

'I didn't . . .'

'Well, all that ink says you did,' grinned Jason. 'Gleaming, mate!'

Liam peeled away the tape and caught sight of himself in the mirrored wall behind the bar. The tattoo was the cap badge of the Rifles Regiment, a bugle horn, under which was inscribed the word 'Rifleman'.

'That greasy stuff is actually nappy cream,' said Jason, knocking Liam from his reflection. 'Works a treat on helping a tattoo heal, apparently.'

Liam's arm stung like he'd been punched with an injection. *Whose stupid idea had it been to come out to Ibiza so soon after getting back from theatre, and then to go and have a tattoo?* he thought. *Oh yeah – mine. Genius.*

Jason grabbed a pint of lager so cold that tiny ice crystals floated in it. He necked it. 'You don't look so well. And by that, I mean you look like crap.'

'Cheers, Finch,' Liam replied, eyes open to stare

bleary-eyed at his companion. 'You always were a bastard.'

'Shut y'face, man,' said Finch, his thick Geordie accent cutting easily through the hum and buzz of the bar. 'You're alive because of me and my awesome ground sight. Don't go forgetting it.'

Liam couldn't respond to that. He'd served alongside Jason for six months in the heat and insanity of Afghanistan. It had been the most exciting, dangerous, terrifying and fantastic time of his life. It was also the saddest, after the loss of his mate, Cameron, courtesy of a well-aimed RPG by the Taliban.

'Ground sight' was a term all soldiers used for keeping a keen eye ahead for anything unusual – and that *anything* could range from an oddly scraped patch of ground to grass bent the wrong way. Jason's ground sight was almost supernatural. Everyone, including Liam, had trusted him implicitly. Yeah, he was cocky about it, but it was allowed. He'd saved more lives than Liam could ever guess at.

'Hangover cure,' said Jason, handing Liam the evil-looking drink. 'Bloody Mary – bloody brilliant!'

Liam may have trusted Jason with his life, but with his stomach he wasn't so sure. 'You a doctor now, then?' he joked. 'You'll need to work on your bedside manner.'

'Shut up and drink up, or sod off.'

Liam took the glass from Finch's hand. The liquid was dark red and thick, and floating in it were bits of celery and cucumber. Ice cubes chinked off the sides of the glass, the sound reminding him of 5.56 cases knocking against each other.

'Hair of the dog and all that, right?' growled Finch.

Liam raised the glass to his lips.

'Drink it, man!'

The first swig and Liam gasped, his breath caught in his throat. His whole face was burning up.

'Bastard!'

Jason shrugged, ordering himself another pint. 'A Bloody Mary needs a kick,' he said, and revealed a small bottle he'd hidden in his left hand. The label showed a red chilli with wings, like the famous SAS dagger insignia.

Liam couldn't speak, just nodded. His face was melting.

'Who Dares Burns,' said Jason with a mischievous wink. 'Hotter than napalm. Love it!'

At last Liam found his voice. 'It's like swallowing lava!' Then, with a deep breath and a shake of his head, he jammed the glass between his lips, ignored the pain and drank the pure fire.

'Get in there!' said Jason, placing his pint of iced lager in front of Liam and clamping him hard on his left shoulder. 'Give it a few minutes, and you'll be raging, mate! Would I lie to you?'

Liam gripped the pint and took a deep, cooling draught. It didn't dampen the pain, but it still felt good. It was a sensation he and the rest of the lads had lusted after on an almost hourly basis while in the relentless heat of Afghanistan.

A shout came from where the bar opened out onto the street, and Liam watched a bloke walk from the bright of the day across to where he and Jason were standing.

'Hi, Chris,' said Liam.

'Christ on a bike, you look crap, Liam.'

'Cheers,' said Liam, gulping more lager. 'Where's the rest of your crew?'

'Unconscious,' said Chris. 'Can't take the pace.'

Chris was part of a group Liam and Jason had bumped into the last couple of nights. A civvie in his early twenties, something in Sales, he said, Chris was out in Ibiza on a stag week. He always called Liam by his first name, whilst in his army life Liam was very used to just being 'Scott!'

'How much did I drink last night?' Liam asked, not really wanting an answer.

'I wouldn't sweat it,' said Chris. 'It's why you're here, right? Hell, if I'd just come back from what you chaps have been doing, I'd be a wreck.'

'Oh, we're broken inside, Chris,' said Jason, and pretended to cry.

Liam laughed. Grim humour was an essential part of dealing with life as a soldier in combat. Even with rounds flying, he'd found himself sharing jokes with his mates. It was a survival mechanism and it worked.

'I'm being serious, though,' said Chris. 'A six-month tour of Afghanistan? That's jolly serious.'

'He's been here five minutes and he's already said "chaps" and "jolly",' smiled Jason. 'Sounds like an officer straight out of Sandhurst!'

For the next hour or two, Liam managed to gradually regain a sense of actually being alive. And Chris was just happy to hang around and listen to their stories. Liam had heard every shitting-into-a-bag, lucky-escape, calling-in-air-support story ever told, had even recounted a few himself. Hearing them again reminded him not only that he liked being in the army, but also that he was already missing being out in theatre.

He had memories of what life had been like before he'd joined. Back then, he'd been drifting, spending most of his time hanging out with a few mates, doing a bit of free running to keep himself busy. His future had seemed far away, too distant to even worry about. Then, one night, his best mate Dan had been killed in a free-running accident. And since that awful moment, so much had changed, had happened, that Liam knew he was different now, and wondered if he'd ever be able to go back – not to how he used to live, but simply to life outside the army.

'Totty, eleven o'clock,' said Chris. By now, the first crowd of drinkers were starting to swarm back into the bar for a Happy Hour that lasted until early evening.

'You sure you've never been to Sandhurst?' asked Jason, glancing over to where Chris was signalling them to join in and have a look. '*Totty* . . . who says that?'

'Me,' said Chris. He placed his empty glass on a nearby table. 'What say we go over there and have a chat?'

Liam made to follow, then looked back at Jason. 'Aren't you supposed to be my point man?'

By the time Liam had got to the girls, Jason had overtaken him and was already deep into a war story.

'So this Terry, right, he's just been taking pot shots at us with this fuckin' RPG, yeah? And then his mates turn up, and suddenly it's getting really fruity . . .'

One of the girls, tall, attractive, and with a permanent look of indifference slapped across her face, said, 'Sounds boring, if you ask me. Do you talk about anything else? Or is it always war and guns and fighting?'

'You're joking, right?' said Liam. 'I'm not saying it's fun, but it's definitely not boring.'

'No one asked you to join up,' she said, sipping from a glass that seemed to hold more fruit on sticks and brightly coloured umbrellas than actual drink. 'Who'd want to be in the army anyway? All that shouting and being ordered about. Seriously dull.'

Liam's mouth fell open. Having only arrived back from Afghanistan two weeks ago, he'd not had much chance or cause to mix with civilians. Not until now, if he was honest. In those two weeks, all he'd really done was sort his kit out – and go to London to collect a medal, the Conspicuous Gallantry Cross. It had been awarded after an action in which he'd been cut off from the rest of his multiple, with another soldier who'd lost his foot to an IED. The Taliban had been hunting them, but Liam had managed to keep them both alive, and evade capture, until they were eventually rescued.

Life in the army had been anything but dull.

'You don't know what you're talking about,' he said, looking at the girl to try and get the measure of her, work out if she was actually serious or not. Then he added with a smile, 'Joining up was the best decision I ever made, period. Wouldn't swap it.'

Liam saw Chris wink at him, then turn to the ladies to let loose his charm offensive.

'Anyway, ladies, what brings you out to Ibiza?

Holiday? Exams over? Or just to have the chance to meet handsome blighters like us?'

The girl with the sour face sneered, but her three friends giggled.

'Let's start as we mean to go on, shall we?' continued Chris. 'Drinks?'

The girls jumped at the chance of free booze, but as they gave Chris their orders, two of them happily exchanging them for a peck on the cheek, Liam was knocked to one side as four lads pushed through to stand with the girls.

'All right, ladies?' said the one who'd glanced against Liam. 'Miss us?'

Liam could tell the girls were unimpressed, even the one who looked like she spent her life sucking lemons.

'We told you to leave us alone last night,' she said. 'And in case you didn't understand, we meant for the rest of the time we're here as well, OK? Just go away.'

'Hey, just relax, babe,' came the reply, dripping with more swarm than charm. 'You don't need to play hard to get. There's still plenty of me to go around, hey, mate?'

The lad winked at Liam and slipped his arm round the girl's waist, pulling her close. He was tall, well groomed, and looked fit, his shirt clearly too small on purpose, just so the girls could get an eyeful of his pecs and biceps.

'I don't think she's playing hard to get,' said Liam. 'Maybe you should just forget it?'

The lad's face turned from cheeky to cheerless in a beat. 'Who the fuck asked you?'

Chris walked over, carrying a tray of drinks, and without a hint of hesitation, the lad reached out and helped himself. 'Cheers, mate!' he said, taking a swig.

'He's not your mate,' said Liam, disliking the new arrivals more with every passing second. 'And that's not your drink.'

The lad let go of the girl and walked over to Liam, still holding the drink. 'Nice haircut,' he said, then clocked the tattoo. 'You a soldier boy, then? A squaddie?'

Liam didn't respond. He'd been warned about people like this. Dickheads who liked to take the piss out of stuff they didn't understand, and who thought the army was an easy target.

The lad stood to attention, then saluted, as his mates laughed and gathered behind him, hyenas behind a wolf.

'We've got ourselves a bona fide war hero here,' he said. 'I bet he's SAS. A killer. Scared, aren't we, eh?'

Jason stepped in. 'Hey, mate, we're not looking for any trouble. So why don't we all just relax, eh? Good times, right?'

The lad ignored him. 'Join the army, huh? Travel the world, meet interesting people, and kill them!'

'We don't do it for fun,' Liam said.

'Don't give a shit what you do it for,' he replied. 'But do me a favour, next time you go out there, step on a land mine or something, yeah? You dull fuck.'

Liam clenched a fist tight. 'You what?'

'A good squaddie is a dead squaddie,' continued the lad, spitting the words at Liam like rounds. 'Least that way we know you've done your fucking job!'

Liam's world shifted. He wasn't in the bar any more. He was back in Afghanistan. Gunfire and explosions and shouts and screams filled his ears. He could smell dust, cordite and blood. And in his arms was Cameron, bleeding out his last few moments of life: a good squaddie – a good friend – soon to be a dead one.

Liam came back online a split second later. Then he heaved Jason out of the way, and let rip.

2

Liam stared at the locker next to his bed. His room was as uncommitted to comfort and individuality as he remembered it: simple wardrobe, a chest of drawers, a sink and a bed. It was perfectly functional and equally soulless. Everything was neat, folded, placed with the kind of precision only someone in the military would understand. After getting back from holiday a week ago, he'd returned straight to barracks. Having picked up a load of new kit from the lance corporal in stores, Liam had finished his ironing, and was now just making sure it was all as it should be, ready to pass any spot inspection the army could throw at him. Back at the start of his training, such attention to detail had seemed a complete waste of time. Now, though, he was proud to see his kit presented so well.

Walking out of his room, he thought back to what had happened in Ibiza – the black eye he had returned with, courtesy of the dipshit in the bar. Losing Cam had been shit, real shit, and it just wasn't that easy when faced with that kind of wanker.

'Hey, Scott! Wait up!'

Liam recognized the voice, obeyed immediately, instinctively. It was Sergeant Reynolds.

'Hey, boss.' He had served under Sergeant Reynolds in Afghanistan, and had come to regard the man – wiry, fit, and with an almost rat-like look to him – as one of the toughest and most fair people he'd ever met.

'So what are you up to?' the sergeant questioned.

'Just sorting stuff out,' said Liam. 'New kit, keeping fit, nothing much really.'

'So, how was leave?' Liam saw him clock the black eye and nod at it. 'Or shouldn't I ask?'

Liam instinctively raised a hand to touch his eye. The area was still tender, and the swelling had come down a lot since arriving back from Ibiza, but the colour had, if anything, got worse.

'I'm guessing you didn't get that out in theatre,' said Reynolds.

'It's OK,' said Liam, lying.

'Bollocks it is,' said Reynolds. 'And you should know better than to try and lie to my face, eh, Scott?'

Liam explained what had happened, and he heard frustration and anger in the sergeant's voice.

'You're a fuckin' idiot, you know that, Scott? Some prick with a gob on him calls you names and you lamp him one? Seriously? Is that what your training's amounted to?'

'He was an arsehole,' said Liam.

'And you're an even bigger one for listening to him, Scott, and you know it!'

'But what he was saying, boss—'

'Doesn't matter,' said Reynolds, cutting Liam off. 'You've seen war first-hand, up close and personal. All that dickhead will have ever done is watch it on the news, or on YouTube.'

Liam said nothing. He knew the sergeant hadn't finished.

'So tell me, Scott, what the hell were you thinking exactly? Because I'm pretty sure making a point with your fists isn't the best way to win someone over and get them to see things from your point of view!'

'He was out of order,' said Liam. As soon as the words were out, he knew just how lame he sounded.

'I didn't train you, work my arse into the muck and dust to keep you alive,' Reynolds said, his words fired at Liam with bullet-like accuracy, 'just to have you come back here and screw it up by getting into a scrape with a random dickhead!'

'No, boss, I know that, but—'

'But what, Scott? *What?* Well?'

Liam said nothing. The sergeant's neck veins were starting to stand out – never a good sign.

'I've been in this job for over twenty years,' said Reynolds, his voice quieter now, which only made it worse. 'I've lost count of the number of lads like you I've seen come through, and I know that with every new recruit who makes it to become a soldier, there's a chance they might not be coming back.'

'I lost my rag,' said Liam. 'I shouldn't have, I know.'

'You need to sort your head out, Scott,' said Reynolds. 'Remember your training, and stay calm. Then walk. The fuck. Away.'

Reynolds paused, clearly, Liam thought, to give him time to think about what had just been said.

The sergeant spoke again. 'If you don't,' he continued, 'you'll screw your own life up, and give the army – and me – a bad reputation. Because if you get upset every time some dicksplash shouts their stupid ignorant views at you, then the best place for you is out, you hear me?'

'Yes, boss,' Liam replied.

'You're a good soldier, Scott,' said Reynolds. 'I should know – I trained you, fought alongside you. That medal was well deserved. And I'm not just saying that to blow smoke up your arse. I'm serious.'

Liam smiled. A compliment from someone like Sergeant Reynolds was hard won. Funny how he made it sound like an insult, nevertheless.

'Thanks, boss.'

'Don't go all Hollywood on me,' said Reynolds. 'Tears I don't do. Just take my advice and make sure that you don't let the few dickheads out there influence how you behave, got me? Don't give them control over who and what you are. You're worth more than that.' He took a deep breath, his face relaxing a little. 'Anyway, that's all I'm going to say. Listen to it or don't, that's your shout. So, you got any plans now you're back?'

Liam shook his head. 'To be honest, I'm just missing it,' he said. 'You know, proper soldiering. Feel like I'm in limbo over here, just kicking around.'

'Get focused,' said Reynolds, turning a suggestion immediately into an order. 'Sort out a training plan. Do some adventure training. Sign up for a course. Keep working on your fitness. You'll be out on tour again in six months and I don't want to chase around some burger-filled arsewipe who's just been sitting on a sofa living on pizza and beer!'

'Is it really that long before a second tour?'

Reynolds nodded.

'That's ages,' said Liam. 'Is there no way I can get out there quicker?'

'You're serious?'

'I know I've only been back here a short time, but out in theatre I felt like I was actually doing something, you know?'

Sergeant Reynolds was quiet for a moment. Then he said, 'You could transfer to 4 Rifles. It's not common, but people do it occasionally. And by *people*, I mean the mad bastards who can't get enough.'

'So 4 Rifles are out sooner?' Liam asked.

'Head out in just a few weeks,' Reynolds replied. 'Our role's changed out there. You'll be working alongside the Afghan National Army, helping them ready up for when we finally bugger off out of their country.'

'They won't take me, though, will they?' said Liam. 'I've just come back.'

Reynolds said, 'You're experienced, Liam. You've been out there, and you know how things work. Your training's been tested. Trust me, they'll snap you up.'

'Really?' asked Liam.

Reynolds grinned. 'You were with me, remember? Best recommendation in the business.'

3

The C17 wasn't exactly luxury air travel, but it did the job, transporting troops and equipment to and from the UK. Fifty-three metres long, and capable of carrying anything from thirteen Land Rovers in one go, to a Chinook helicopter, it was also fitted out for up to 102 passengers. Liam knew that in a few minutes, before the aircraft started its descent to Camp Bastion, the internal lights would be switched off, and it would be dark inside the aircraft too. The last time he had gone through this, flying through Afghanistan's air space and into Camp Bastion, seemed a lifetime ago, yet it was little more than eight months. So much had happened in that time that Liam knew he was a different person now in almost every way possible. And it felt good.

He remembered the mix of nerves and excitement, the sense of heading off into the unknown. This time he was still nervous, still excited, but in a different way.

He knew what to expect, fully understood the risks and the danger because he'd already experienced it, and in some ways that was reassuring. He knew what lay ahead of him, as unpredictable and potentially deadly as it was, and he also knew that his skills and training would give him every chance to survive it.

With Camp Bastion only half an hour away, everyone was wearing their helmets and body armour. As the plane lights went off, they sat in total darkness, a darkness which was treacle-thick and ripe with expectation, excitement and fear.

A few moments later, the plane banked hard left.

'Shit . . .'

It was the soldier next to Liam. When they'd climbed onto the plane, Liam had noticed that he was probably the smallest bloke among them. And judging by what he'd just said, his voice breaking with nervous anticipation, he was also new. They'd said their hellos, given names, but Liam had forgotten it the moment it was spoken. He guessed the soldier was about the same age as himself, but he looked younger, his blond hair and pale face making him resemble the Milky Bar Kid. Liam had seen the soldier fiddling with a keyring in the shape of a rugby ball and he felt pretty sure that this must be his first tour. For him, that brought back a lot of memories. He knew exactly what the soldier was going through.

'The pilot's putting the plane into a spiral manoeuvre,' he explained. 'Means we're not so easy to hit if any Taliban are out there bored and looking to have a pot shot with an RPG.'

'That's not making me feel any better,' said the soldier.

He had a point, thought Liam. He decided that changing the subject might help keep him calm. 'I'm Scott,' he said again. 'Sorry – I got your name earlier, but I'm shit with names.'

'Martin, I mean Saunders,' said the soldier.

Liam smiled. 'You ready to jump?'

'What? How do you mean? Jump from what?'

'The plane doesn't land,' said Liam, not expecting to get far with this leg-pull. 'We jump, remember? You were briefed on it, surely.'

Martin was quiet.

'Parachutes are under our seats.'

Though Liam could only really make out the faint shadow of Saunders' silhouette, he saw him dip forward to check.

'Shit . . .'

Liam left it a moment, then laughed. 'Sorry, mate, couldn't resist it; can't believe you actually checked! Brilliant!'

'Bastard . . .' hissed Martin.

'Didn't think you'd believe me, to be honest.'

'Not a fan of flying,' said Martin. 'It's not natural, us being up here.' He took a deep breath, then said, 'How come you're out here again so soon? Haven't you just got back?'

Liam explained how he'd transferred to 4 Rifles so that he could get back to soldiering rather than waiting around for his next tour. It was a decision he hadn't yet regretted.

'You missed it that much?'

'Better than anything I'd been doing with my life before I joined up,' said Liam.

Martin said, 'You're that lad from 2 Rifles who got a medal, right?'

Liam said nothing. He was proud of it, but hardly spoke about what had happened. Didn't seem right. But word had got round, as it tended to. The army was, in many ways, just one big family, albeit a dysfunctional one of epic proportions.

'I recognized you when I sat down,' said Saunders. 'Sounds like you had a hell of a time out here.'

'I just did what any soldier would do in the same situation,' Liam said. 'Your training kicks in, and you just get on with what you have to do. Everyone who comes here deserves a medal.'

Martin said, 'You should be proud of it.'

'I am,' Liam replied. 'But I'm not going to shout my head off about it. I was hardly thinking *There's a medal in this* when everything was kicking off.'

The plane was still on its steep spiral. Camp Bastion was only minutes away now. Liam was actually excited.

'What's it like? Bastion, I mean?' Martin asked.

'Massive,' said Liam. 'It's like a town more than a camp.'

Martin was quiet, then said, 'Pretty much shitting myself. Feel like I'm eleven and heading off to secondary school.'

And you don't look much older, thought Liam, hiding a smile.

'Nerves are good,' he said. 'I'd be more worried if you weren't scared.'

'Easy for you to say,' said Martin.

'It's the truth,' Liam replied. 'If you're not nervous, then you're not alert to what might happen. You can use it to your advantage.'

An announcement from the pilot echoed through the plane: they were coming in to land.

'Ready?' asked Liam.

'Hope so,' said Martin.

The pilot's voice came back on line. 'Thank you for flying with us and have a lovely holiday. Welcome to Costa Afghanistan!'

* * *

Landing done, the thick darkness of the Afghanistan night kept at bay only by the torches they all carried, Liam walked in line from the plane into familiar air, a mix of desert heat, hot vehicles, dust and sweat. There was a distant tang of more unpleasant smells, courtesy of the huge effluent pools, or shit pits, kept at bay by regular burning.

The heat was as he'd remembered: like stepping out of an igloo and into a furnace, even at this time of night. Camp Bastion itself was unlit after dusk so it was perilous to walk around. A major hazard was the numerous vehicles trundling around the place, most of them capable of crushing you into the ground without noticing.

After collecting his kit, Liam, with a group of others, was taken to his new quarters – a simple metal-framed temporary building, lined with folding beds and accompanying mosquito nets.

The room, if such a place could be called that, was all function, with nothing in the way of comfort or welcome. Dust-covered matting did its best to provide a level floor, but the desert ground underneath was playing a different game and stepping carefully was the only way to avoid tripping up. The colour scheme was various shades of beige, with a bit of grey and brown thrown in.

Laying out his doss bag, Liam quickly got himself and his kit in order. It didn't take long, and seeing his weapons laid out neat and tidy was another sign that he really was back out in Afghanistan. Back home, weapons were locked away for good reason. In theatre, they were by your side, the reasons just as good.

As he got himself sorted, Liam shared nods and grunts of weary greeting with the other lads. Liam knew them by face but little else. He was still new and playing catch-up with names.

Martin was opposite him and was engrossed in sorting his kit like he was back at Catterick and fearing a bollocking from a grumpy NCO. A couple of the other lads were clearly seasoned soldiers, and probably, thought Liam, more so than he himself.

Another soldier caught Liam's attention. Older than the rest – probably around forty, Liam guessed – with greying hair cut short where it wasn't already receding. He had photos out from home of his family, a wife and two young children: a boy and a girl. Liam gave a nod, which was returned then followed up by a jog over.

'Eastwood, right?' said Liam, working to remember names and faces from the build-up training.

'Yep,' said the soldier. 'I'll let you guess my first name.'

'Scott,' said Liam, introducing himself. 'And it can't be.'

'Oh, it is! Dad was a huge Western fan. His favourite films were *High Plains Drifter* and *Pale Rider*.'

Liam grinned at the thought of growing up with the same name as Hollywood legend Clint Eastwood, who made his name being a hardass cowboy on the silver screen in films like *The Good, the Bad and the Ugly*. 'You carry a Peacemaker?' he asked, remembering the famous revolver Clint had used in so many Westerns.

'Pacemaker, more like,' said one of the others, a tall, pointy-faced lad called Ade Sunter who was reading a well-thumbed climbing magazine through bleary eyes. He was fiddling with a karabiner, a metal clip used in climbing as well as to clip kit to bergens. 'Old bastard. You bring the zimmer frame then, Cowboy?'

Clint laughed. 'I've had worse nicknames,' he said. He turned back to Liam. 'So how are you feeling being out here again so quick? Made the right decision? This is my third tour, but I didn't exactly want to jump the queue like you did.'

'How did you know?' asked Liam.

'You're the lad who transferred,' said Clint. 'Everyone knows. You liked it that much, right?'

'Loved it,' said Liam.

'Young and keen,' said Clint.

Ade called over with, 'Better than being old and shit. You able to draw your pension over here, or what?'

As Clint laughed, Liam was momentarily acutely aware not just of his age, but his inexperience. Clint had by his own admission done two tours, and it was obvious Ade had been out as often if not more.

Martin joined them.

'Hey, it's Mascot!' said Clint.

'Sod off, Cowboy,' said Martin, and Liam could tell he was doing his best to sound as much the soldier as the rest of them. It was almost convincing, though Clint's nickname came out a little forced.

'Mascot?' asked Liam.

'He's here to bring us good luck,' said Clint. 'Not only is he about the size of something hanging from a charm bracelet, he also carries around that little rugby ball keyring like a magic rabbit's foot.'

Martin laughed. He was clearly used to the ribbing.

'I've seen children bigger,' continued Clint. 'Actually, I've got two of my own that actually are. And they're only six and eight years old!'

Liam glanced at the photographs Clint had put out. 'Can't imagine being a dad,' he said.

'No one can, until you become one,' said Clint.

The second of the other two soldiers, a stocky bloke in his mid-twenties called Rob Hammond who, Liam had noticed, spent most of his time plugged into his iPod, called over, 'If you rub his head, he'll grant you a wish. Before I met him, I was as ugly as Clint, but look at me now! Thanks, Mascot!'

Everyone laughed. But then Rob wasn't exactly a looker, and knew it, which was half the joke. His face bore the scars of years spent boxing, and his hands looked fit to rip through walls. Like everyone, his hair was cut short, but it was so black and thick it made him look like his head was covered in Velcro.

'He might even be able to sort out that tattoo of yours, Scott,' Rob added. 'Were you drunk when you had that done?'

'Yes, and it's not that bad, is it?'

Rob didn't get a chance to answer as footsteps interrupted them.

'Hello, gents.'

It was a voice Liam was already getting used to hearing, that of Corporal Cowell, one of the NCOs out with 4 Rifles. Even though he'd only been with the regiment a short length of time, Liam had quickly realized that Cowell was one grumpy bastard.

'Corporal,' everyone responded instantly, their voices bumping into each other.

If there was one thing that made the corporal stand out, thought Liam, it was that he was always, and without fail, impeccably dressed. Even his face seemed to be shiny, like he polished that too. In his thirties, the NCO was as tall as any of them, and carried the build of someone who spent most evenings throwing weights around. Not that he was muscle-bound, just big and hard-looking. He reminded Liam of a bulldog.

'All settling in, lads?'

'Yes, Corporal,' everyone chimed.

'What about you, Saunders?' the corporal asked. 'These experienced wankers filling your head with their tosspot war stories yet?'

'No, Corporal,' Martin answered.

'Well, do yourself a favour and don't listen to a single word they say,' said the corporal, like Martin's answer was completely and utterly inconsequential. 'Half of it is bravado, the other half bullshit.' His face didn't so much move as slide from Martin to stare at Liam. 'Isn't that right, Scott, hey? Bullshit and bravado?'

Liam was caught off guard, not least because this was the first time Corporal Cowell had actually spoken to him directly.

'Yes, Corporal,' he said, not really thinking about what he was actually saying, just replying on auto.

The others laughed. Liam tried to, but his face wasn't into it, almost like his muscles had to be forced to move into the right position. Why was Corporal Cowell singling him out? Was he getting at him somehow? Implying that his medal, his own experiences, were like he'd just said: simply bullshit and bravado?

No, that couldn't be it, thought Liam. *He's just doing his job. Doesn't want Saunders listening to everyone else and thinking this is all guns-a-blazing, like in the movies.* And that was fair enough. Still, it did put his guard up a little.

The corporal marched away, his steps measured and smart. Then, just before he left, he turned back into the room and said, 'Focus on your training, lads, you hear? You're not over here to collect glory stories. You're here to do a job, and get home alive. That's all that matters. Got me?'

No one said anything until the corporal had left.

'Fucking X-Factor is a right twat,' said Ade. 'He's all spit, polish and no fucking balls.'

Liam laughed; he thought the nickname for the corporal was one of the better ones he'd heard.

'You swear a lot,' said Clint.

'So fucking what?' Ade replied, the karabiner still clicking away in his hand.

'Just an observation.'

It hadn't escaped Liam's attention that Clint, as yet, hadn't sworn once. And that was weird. They were soldiers. It was how they communicated.

'You do talk some bollocks,' said Ade.

'And yet still we understand each other,' said Clint.

As Clint and Ade both laughed, Liam sat down on his bed. Uncomfortable as it was, at that very moment, it felt like the best bed in the world. This was where he belonged.

4

Bastion was a monster that never slept. Liam, walking to grab some breakfast, noticed how silence and quiet were alien things in this place, the air constantly humming with voices and engines and aircraft.

Near the mess tent, a Wolfhound trundled past. The thrum of the six-wheeled vehicle shook the ground and sent up great clouds of pink-grey dust. Highly protected, and armed with a 7.62 general-purpose machine gun, or 'Gimpy', the Wolfhound was heavy, hard and ugly, and was used in the main to carry vital combat supplies, such as water and ammunition, for front-line patrols. Liam fancied driving one. But then that was one of the great things about being in the army: the kit. There was always something new to have a go at, some extra training to hook in to.

It was his second morning in RSOI – Reception, Staging, and Onward Integration – a process of acclimatization that focused on getting those troops newly out in Afghanistan used to what life was going to be like while they were out on tour. It might have been only a few weeks since he was last out, but for Liam it was still a shock to the system.

The size of Bastion itself was breath-taking: a town in the desert, but with everyone working for the same employer, to all intents and purposes wearing the same uniform. Liam had already noticed one big difference since his last tour, though: all the fast food joints had gone. Liam wasn't too bothered, but Rob was not impressed.

'Not a decent burger or pizza place anywhere,' he grumbled, piling up his plate with enough breakfast for three. 'How the hell are we supposed to eat?'

'Blame the Americans,' said Liam. 'I heard that a US general wasn't massively impressed with troops getting fat on fast food.'

The general, so Liam had been told, had demanded action after finding a few less than able grunts stuffing their faces with pizza. So out went the fast food and in came even more gym equipment, along with an endless supply of fitness supplements. If there's one thing the Americans knew how to do, thought Liam, it was throw money at a problem until it either went away or just drowned in dollar signs.

Sitting down at a table, Hammond continued to grumble as he pushed toast into his face. It was like watching someone feed a loaf of bread into a garbage disposal unit.

Clint nodded at Hammond's tray.

'Three fried eggs? Well, you know what they say, Hammond? You are what you eat.'

Hammond laughed. 'Too right they do, Cowboy, and you know what? I don't remember ever eating a fucking legend!'

Liam decided to remember that line – it was one of Hammond's best, even if it wasn't exactly accurate.

Despite it being early in the day, and them all being inside a large mess tent, the heat was already suffocating. Greased up with sun cream, and sweating, their clothes stuck to them; the tang of BO lingered in the air permanently, mixing with the aromas drifting in from the kitchen. It wasn't pleasant, but it was all part of the experience, and Liam was enjoying it. Unlike the last time he'd arrived at Bastion, RSOI was now carried out at a dedicated facility within the camp, which included an Afghan compound to provide realistic training, a driver training centre, and a couple of Roll Over Drill and Egress Training mechanisms (RODET) to practise escape techniques if a vehicle rolled on patrol.

But it was later that morning, breakfast duly demolished, that Liam had some real fun when he got the opportunity to use a new weapon only recently deployed with the troops – the L129A1 Sharpshooter.

'These are for use by the best shots in the infantry,' a corporal running the shooting range told him, cradling the weapon with something akin to fatherly love. 'So don't fuck this up.'

Liam was a good shot. He wasn't big-headed about it, but it was the truth, something he'd increasingly realized during his last tour. It was a skill all soldiers respected, for obvious reasons. Handling a weapon that would help him test his skills even further was exciting.

'The whole point of this new weapon,' the corporal explained, 'is to improve long-range firepower in theatre. Taking a 7.62 round, the Sharpshooter will be able to hit a target up to eight hundred metres, which is a bit fucking different to the standard issue SA80.'

Liam was impressed by what he'd heard of the weapon, and even more so after laying down some rounds with it. *Accurate* didn't seem an adequate word to describe how it handled. The weapon's accuracy was enhanced by the fitting of the Advanced Combat Optical Gunsight (ACOG), which Liam had used a few times before heading back out to Afghanistan. That and the Lightweight Day Sight (LDS) were replacing the older SUSAT sights and were significantly more capable. The ACOG itself provided up to 6x fixed power magnification, was significantly lighter than the SUSAT, and was illuminated at night by an internal phosphor. There was also no getting away from the fact that, despite its deadly purpose and fearsome capability, the weapons system as a package looked seriously impressive.

With the first two days of RSOI done, Liam pushed on through the rest of the training. This covered dealing with Improvised Explosive Devices (IEDs), working as a patrol, understanding Afghan culture, and vehicle drills. He also practised clearing compounds and using heavy weapons systems.

After a day of numerous compound clearance drills, Liam was with Martin outside one of the coffee shops the American general had deemed safe enough not to tear down and send back home. The addiction to caffeine, Liam thought, was probably encouraged, if only to keep soldiers awake enough to survive the long and exhausting hours.

'What do you think it's going to be like working with the ANA?' Martin asked.

'They're just soldiers,' said Liam. 'Doing a job like us. That's it.'

'But what about the insider attacks?' asked Martin, and Liam heard the concern in his voice.

Insider attacks weren't common, but they had all heard that there were more each month. The Taliban always considered it a real coup to get someone in under the radar. They would target someone in the ANA, threaten their family, and force them to switch sides; then that was it, they had an armed soldier working alongside ISAF forces with no choice but to open fire.

During his last tour, Liam remembered the sense of being wary of all Afghans. Fair or not, it was a case of self-preservation. Everyone knew someone who knew someone who'd been smashed apart by an IED, or shot, killed even, and no one was taking any chances.

'What happens if something kicks off?' said Martin. 'What if I don't clock something's up and it all goes to shit?' Without even pausing for breath, he continued, 'There was one last week. Afghan soldier at an FOB emptied his mag on our soldiers. Wounded four. That could happen again, couldn't it? Right?'

Liam had heard about the incident. 'Just have to depend on your training,' he said. 'Stay alert.'

'Doesn't make me feel any better about heading out to our FOB,' Martin replied.

'Just focus on your job. That's all you need to worry about, trust me.'

Martin pulled out a small booklet from a pocket. 'I keep reading through this, trying to memorize it, but none of it's sticking!'

It was a Pashto phrase book. Army issue, and handed to all soldiers in theatre, it came with a phrase book for Dari, the language spoken in the north from where most of the ANA were recruited. The books were useful, thought Liam, who was keen to do his best to learn both languages, but the pictures inside looked like they'd been copied from a rubbish Afghanistan-themed computer game. The one of the thief was particularly bad – a man running with a sack on his back. All that was missing was a mask over his eyes.

'It'll make more sense when you use it with some locals,' said Liam, trying to reassure Martin. 'It gets easier when you use it in context. You just need to practise.'

Martin remained quiet.

'You probably know more of it than you realize,' said Liam, focusing on the Pashto rather than confusing Martin even more with Dari. 'What would you say if I said, "*Salaamu alaikum*"?'

Martin paused then said, '*Walaikam salum?*'

'Close,' said Liam. '*Walaikum salaam*. What about "*Tsunga ye*"?'

'*Za sha yam?*' Martin replied hesitantly.

'Spot on!'

'Really?'

Liam opened the first page of the phrase book and pointed at what they'd just said.

'I asked, "How are you" and you replied with "I am fine". Great!'

'I guess.'

'Just do a little a day,' said Liam. 'We'll practise together if you want. I need it as much as you do.' At that, Liam saw Martin visibly relax. Standing up he said, 'I'm going to head to the gym. You coming?'

'*Hoo*,' Martin replied with a grin, clearly chuffed he'd remembered the Pashto word for *yes*.

Numerous gyms were dotted around the camp. Filled with state-of-the art equipment, they were always busy. With little else to do to relax around camp, body-building, weights and fitness were activities that passed the time, and also allowed you to let off some steam. As they entered the nearest gym, Martin knocked Liam on the arm and pointed.

'Cowboy,' said Martin.

Away from all the main gym equipment, the free weights and smiths press machines, and everything else needed to get the veins popping and sweat running, was an area of clear floor space. Hanging from the wall were some skipping ropes, a pull-up bar, and on the floor a few sit-up mats and some press-up bars. Hanging from the pull-up bar was Clint. He was doing pull-ups and, Liam noticed, somewhat effortlessly.

'One of the fittest in 4 Rifles,' said Martin. 'When he turned up some of the others took the piss because he was TA. They reckoned he wouldn't even survive our pre-deployment training.'

Liam watched as Clint dropped from the bar to the floor to hammer out some perfectly executed press-ups.

'What happened?' he asked.

'Nothing,' said Martin. 'Cowboy doesn't get easily riled up, as you've probably noticed. He just sat quiet, then destroyed everyone in the fitness tests. And by destroyed, I mean he nuked every fucker there.'

Liam smiled. He could just imagine Clint enjoying that.

'To be honest,' said Martin, 'most of the TA lads are as fit, if not fitter, than the regulars.'

'They probably have to work harder at it,' said Liam. 'They do this as well as a normal job. Nutters, if you ask me.'

Knackered after a decent workout that had involved not just the free weights, but a cross-trainer and rowing machine, Liam and Martin bumped into Clint as they were leaving.

'For an old bastard, you're in serious shape,' Liam said.

'I don't just keep fit for this,' said Clint, as they made their way back to their quarters. 'I run some self-defence stuff back home.'

'You mean all that ninja stuff?' asked Martin, his eyes wide.

Clint shook his head. 'Reality-based training,' he said. 'It's not really a martial art – that stuff's no use in a real fight in the street. What I teach is how to identify a threat, deal with it, and get away sharpish. Not how to score points in a competition.'

Liam was impressed. He was about to ask if Clint could teach them a few basic moves when Corporal Cowell walked up.

'Been training, lads?'

'Yes, Corporal,' Liam and Clint acknowledged.

'Good,' came the short reply. 'See you at the Company Briefing later.'

Then he was gone.

'A man of few words, is X-Factor,' said Clint.

Liam still hadn't worked the corporal out. 'Always acts like he's back in training,' he said. 'Reminds me of what life was like back at Harrogate and Catterick. Always being shouted at by NCOs.'

Clint laughed.

'What?' asked Liam. 'Did I say something funny?'

'That's all X-Factor's ever done,' said Clint. 'You probably don't know, because you're new to 4 Rifles, but Corporal Cowell has spent his career in training posts. The other NCOs all have experience of being in theatre. Cowell, though? This is his first tour. He's as new as you, Saunders.'

Liam stopped mid-stride. 'You mean he's never been in theatre? In combat?'

Clint shook his head. Slowly.

'He's as green as me?' said Martin, letting out a long, deliberate breath. 'Shit . . .'

Clint said nothing.

5

It was forty-three degrees in the shade. Camp Bastion, Liam knew from experience, was plush compared with any FOB they could be sent to, with showers and decent food, but it still provided no escape from the searing, relentless heat. All anyone could do was keep covered up and drink water, and that meant litres of the stuff every day.

Dehydration was dealt with by drinking your own bodyweight in water on a daily basis. Most soldiers didn't just take a camel bak – a special backpack that contained a hydration system – out on patrol, they had one with them most of the time, usually a lightweight model used by runners, plus a bottle of water to hand at all times. Liam had even spotted a few attempts at modern art around the camp: sculptures built by bored soldiers entirely from used plastic water bottles.

Liam's legs were already in bits thanks to a morning spent completing a punishing five-kilometre run in battle kit, followed by some time down on the range with his SA80. The run hadn't been tough because of the distance; back home he could hammer through 5K barely breaking into a sweat. But in Afghanistan things were different. The heat was monstrous, and the sweat didn't just make your clothes stick to you, it sucked up the dust in the air and turned it into a sort of glue. And as the day wore on, it turned into a crust you could peel off like a layer of skin.

As for hygiene and cleanliness, you just had to do your best. And so long as you were vigilant in keeping your doss area clean, had regular showers and washed properly, then that was the best you could do.

Now, though, Liam was running up and down a dusty pock-marked pitch, the boundary marked by stones, trying to work out what rugby was all about. He'd never played it before in his life.

The ball appeared out of nowhere on an intercept course with his head. Liam's instinct was to duck, but he'd realized already that all this did was get him booed at by everyone else playing the game. So he jumped in the air and, to his surprise, caught it. Clasping it under his arm, he did the only thing he knew how to do, and that was run. Not pass it, not look around for anyone on his team, just hammer his legs hard, muscles working like engine pistons, to get him to the touchline.

Liam heard the shouts of everyone else on the pitch. What they wanted him to do, he hadn't the faintest idea. So he pushed the voices out of his head and sped on.

The touchline was close now. Someone tried to pull him to the ground, but he had momentum and that carried him through. Then his sixth sense kicked in. It had helped numerous times out on patrol, and all soldiers spoke about it. An additional sense that everything quite soon was going to go to shit.

Someone was on his tail and he couldn't shake them. But it was just a few metres more. He could make it. Had to. Then arms wrapped around his legs with the strength of steel cable, took his feet from under him, and he was suddenly flying horizontal through the air. The ground came up quick, hammering into Liam, stealing his breath. The ball bounced from his arm. He looked up. The touchline was barely a hand's reach away.

'You're a bloody good runner.'

Liam looked up to see a hand reaching down. He grabbed it and was on his feet. 'Mascot?' He was stunned. The smallest bloke in the battalion, if not the entire army, had taken him out as effectively as a Stinger missile.

Martin grinned, his face dusty and a bit bloodied. He

was clearly in his element. 'Rugby's the best game on the planet! Way better than that football bollocks. All those pretty boys prancing about. Who wants that? Fucking pointless.'

'You don't look . . .' Liam's voice dried up in his mouth from the dust and the heat and the exertion.

'Big enough?' Martin finished for him.

Liam shrugged, nodded.

Martin laughed and jogged off to get back in the game.

That evening, it was the Company Briefing. They'd heard it all before, not just since being at the FOB, but before flying out. They all knew what they would be doing once beyond the perimeter of Camp Bastion, but being told again was sensible. It ensured everyone was absolutely clear.

Liam was sitting with the rest of 4 Rifles. In front of them were the officers and NCOs. Liam already knew that once out of Bastion he would be under a young officer, Lieutenant Steers, a shining example of all that was good about Officer Training Centre Sandhurst; a gnarly, stocky sergeant called Miller, who had the look of a bar brawler about him; Corporal Cowell; and Lance Corporal Clark, a Fijian giant who looked capable of hammering mountains into rubble. However, the only one he really knew yet was Cowell. They'd had briefings already, and he'd done training with all of them, but it was Cowell he so far seemed to keep running into.

The highest-ranking officer there was Major Varley, a man with piercing eyes and a voice that rang with unshakeable determination and personal drive as he took the floor.

'As you are all aware,' he began, 'we shall soon be heading into the Yakchal Valley. And the best way to describe it is that it is very much a heart of darkness.'

Liam knew he wasn't the only one sitting there who didn't much like that description.

'The Yakchal has created a number of key players in the Taliban. The Afghan National Army is now fully taken up with securing the main route through the area, Highway One. Our job is to support the ANA in their work to the very best of our ability.'

The major spoke as though fully confident that no one could ever disagree with him. It was as reassuring as it was unnerving. His calm, focused approach and the way he enunciated each and every word demonstrated how important even the smallest details were to him. He also had an uncanny talent for remembering names and clearly prided himself on knowing his men.

'The insurgency in that area has never been fully defeated,' continued the major. 'We aim to change that.

Our mission, just so that we are all clear, is not to go out looking for a scrap. We will work in an advisory capacity alongside the ANA to help them clear the Taliban out for good and make the area safe. The ANA have their own fully manned patrol bases in the area. We will be supporting them in their work, carrying out regular patrols, improving relations with the local population and, where insurgents are found, ensuring that they decide to leave.'

Liam was impressed with the major's masterful use of understatement.

'We will lead by example,' said the major, drawing to a close. 'We will set a high bar, and I will expect us all to reach it on an individual as well as team basis.'

The major stepped back and Sergeant Miller came forward.

'Right,' said Miller, 'now that you all understand what we'll actually be doing, you'll be pleased to hear that in a few days we can all get the fuck out of Bastion and get on with it.'

Liam smiled. What Major Varley had in finesse, Sergeant Miller had in being blunt. The sergeant was an experienced soldier, a born warrior. Badged as a paratrooper, as well as a sniper, he had been through a number of tours, including ones in Eastern Europe and Iraq, as well as Afghanistan. The very obvious scar on his face – a jagged rip down his left cheek, from his eye to his chin – carried with it lots of speculation. Liam wasn't sure which of the stories to believe, if any of them. All anyone knew was that it had happened in combat, up close and personal. And that was enough. More than. They all practised it, but no one really wanted to think about, and most definitely not experience, the true horror of driving the war home with the point of a bayonet, staring into the eyes of someone you've just killed.

Miller spoke again. 'It's all very well having hot showers, nice gyms, good food and all that bollocks, but that's not why we are here. This is not fucking Butlin's and I can assure you all that I am most definitely not a sodding Redcoat. You're all here to do a job. Proper soldiering. And trust me when I tell you that when you do it, you will do it better than any other fucker out here. You should be proud to be a part of 4 Rifles. So work hard, do your job, and get home safe. That's all I ask.'

The sergeant paused, then added, 'Well, that, and if things kick off, to fight like a mad bastard and survive. Right?'

Everyone chorused with a 'Yes, Sergeant.'

Liam was warming to Miller. He was tough and driven and, from Liam's own experience out in theatre, that was exactly what he wanted from a sergeant. Someone whom he could trust in a fight. This was a man he wanted to be alongside when the inevitable happened and they ended up in a scrap with the Taliban.

Miller asked, 'Any questions?'

Clint raised a hand.

'Eastwood?'

'What's the situation like out on the ground? Do we know what we can expect to be facing?'

It was Cowell who answered. 'Take a wild guess, Eastwood,' he said. 'The Taliban! You've all seen the intelligence. They're out there and they're always working on ways to hit us, big and small. Pot shots with a blast from an AK, snipers, RPGs, IEDs. Whatever the fuck they can think of and get their hands on.'

'Just wondered if things had changed at all,' Clint continued. 'Some are saying the Taliban have cleared off and the biggest danger is IEDs. Others are saying this is just a bit of calm before we walk in and everyone comes in to have a go. Are the Rules of Engagement any different if we're not actively searching out the—'

'Just focus on getting your kit in order, and your mind right,' said Cowell, cutting Clint off sharper than a razor. 'The situation on the ground changes all the time. You know that, Eastwood. Anything else?'

Clint shrugged and sat back. Liam raised his hand.

'What is it, Scott?'

'When I was out here a couple of months back it didn't seem like the Taliban were backing off at all,' he said. 'We were getting hammered every day. I'd rather know what we're up against.'

Corporal Cowell's face turned fierce as he stared back at Liam. 'We all know you were out here,' he said, his voice dripping with barely disguised contempt, 'and about what you did, but things change quickly in warfare, Scott. That's all you need to know.'

'But—'

Cowell stared Liam down.

After a few more questions, Major Varley once again took the floor to close down the brief. This time, though, his finesse with language was replaced with a matter-of-fact abruptness. He wasn't messing around.

'Be aware, all of you, that beyond those walls are people who want you dead,' he said. And he allowed his eyes to travel across the troops in front of him. 'Some of them even treat it like a holiday; working for half the year, in their own country, then heading out here for the killing season. They're seasoned fighters and they know what they're doing.'

Liam couldn't get his head around the kind of person who'd hold a normal job down, then come out here for a few months to just kill. Then back home after for hugs and kisses from the wife and kids, Saturday night TV, and a nice dinner.

'Don't let this place make you go soft,' continued Varley. 'When you're out there you need to be one hundred per cent alert, doing your job, and thinking of nothing else.'

He took a breath. No one spoke.

'So between now and when we head out, sort your personal stuff out good and proper. Write home. Tell people you love them. Sort out your death letters. I'm not saying it to be heartless, I'm saying it because it needs to be said. Right? Good. See you all tomorrow.'

Liam walked back to his quarters with Martin and Clint. He found himself already wishing for some moisture in the air. It was the one thing everyone complained about back home – the rain, the damp, the lack of sunshine. But when all you had was the blast of furnace-like heat, day in, day out, you soon realized just how lucky the UK was. That damp in the air made the world smell more alive, rather than dead like dry tinder. And rain meant plant life, green; a colour almost entirely absent in the grubby terrain of Afghanistan. Ade and Rob headed off on their own somewhere else, both complaining that what they could really do with was a good night out on the piss.

'Heart of darkness,' said Martin. 'Doesn't sound inviting, does it?'

For a few paces, no one replied. Around them, the dark of the evening was stretching out fingers of gloom from the horizon. The heat had abated a little, but it hadn't yet died completely. Liam noticed how the day smelled different when it closed, like the weak remnants of a barbecue holding onto its dying heat, still rich with fat and burned meat.

'Miller's got it together, though,' said Liam, holding open the door to their room. 'He's someone you want on your side when you go somewhere dangerous.'

Martin didn't reply.

'We're all nervous,' said Liam, sensing Martin's unvoiced nerves. 'Even Cowboy!'

Clint laughed as he ducked through into the dormitory. 'What are you implying?'

'It's weird,' said Martin. 'I'm half excited and half so bloody scared I want to throw up.'

'That's normal,' said Clint. 'If you felt anything else I'd be telling you to go home. What we do is scary. You can't escape that. All you can do is learn to deal with it. And you will.'

Walking into their temporary home Liam found himself remembering when, during his last tour, things had got so desperate that they had thought their compound was going to be overrun. They were ordered to destroy any personal effects that could identify them or anyone connected to them. It had been terrifying, facing the prospect not just of hand-to-hand combat, but possible capture, torture and a horrific death.

As Clint followed him in, with Martin behind, Liam had an idea that might boost Martin's confidence a little.

'So how's about teaching us some of that self-defence stuff you do?' he asked, looking at Clint. 'Wouldn't do us any harm, would it? You know, to know a couple of moves.'

Clint hesitated. 'Look,' he said. 'It's not judo or karate, right?'

'What is it then?' asked Martin.

'Effective is what it is,' said Clint and gestured Liam to the centre of where they were bunked. 'And you, Mascot. May as well join in.'

Martin made to protest, but was soon up with Liam and Clint.

'First rule,' said Clint, 'is to identify the threat, right?'

'Such as?' asked Liam.

'Could be anything,' said Clint. 'Could be someone following you, a loudmouth at a pub coming on to your girlfriend or someone yelling and backing you into a corner. Your job is to be alert enough to work out what's happening, then react before they've got a chance to do what it is they want to do.'

'Like what—?'

Liam was given no chance to finish speaking. Clint grabbed him round the neck and pinned him to a locker.

'What you going to do, Liam? What? Come on!'

Liam was surprised and panicked. Clint was usually calm, collected, kindly even. Now, though, there was a meanness in his eye and it told Liam that beneath the relaxed exterior was an utter bastard when things turned nasty. They were fighter's eyes, and Liam knew in that moment that they'd seen a few.

He immediately went with both hands to his neck to drag off Clint's own hand. It wouldn't budge.

Clint let go.

'Fuck me,' said Liam. 'You could've given me a warning.'

'Why?' asked Clint. 'Is a mugger going to warn you? What if we're overrun – is a member of the Taliban going to tell you what they're going to do next?'

'Fair point,' said Liam.

'Good,' said Clint. 'Now let me show you what you should've done. Grab my neck.'

Liam did as he was told.

'Don't be soft,' said Clint. 'Grab it!'

Liam gripped hard.

'What's the threat, Martin?'

'Choking?'

Clint nodded. 'But what about his spare hand? For all I know he's packing a knife, a pistol, a bottle, anything to do me damage. So I need to do two things, preferably simultaneously: defend, and attack.'

Clint hooked a hand round Liam's wrist. At the same time as snapping it away from his own throat, he sent a flurry of punches past Liam's head with his other fist. Then he dragged Liam down, dummy kicking him in the groin, dropped him to the floor, checked left and right, and ran to the far end of the space they were standing in.

'It's not about being fancy,' said Clint, walking back. 'It's about doing the minimum needed with brutal force, staying alive, and getting away sharpish.'

Liam was impressed. 'Show me again?'

Clint started to reply, but a distant, dull thud from outside stopped him dead. It was a sound Liam recognized in an instant.

'That was a mortar,' he said.

'It can't be!' said Martin. 'We're in Bastion!'

'Makes fuck all difference to the Taliban,' said Liam.

Another thud, louder.

'And that was closer.'

'Any closer and you might hear me swear,' said Clint.

The joke lightened the moment, but it was short-lived as another thud hammered in.

The ground shook. Dust burst from every corner and surface as shelves unloaded themselves onto the floor, weapons clattered to the ground and Liam got clonked on the head by one of Clint's family photographs.

'Shit, is this for real?' asked Martin, a nervous laugh escaping his lips.

Then Liam heard another sound, so faint it was almost impossible to detect. But he knew it was there, knew Clint had heard it: a whistle of something cutting through the air.

'Incoming!' he yelled.

With nowhere to hide, Liam dropped to the floor, heard Clint and Martin do the same.

Then everything went black.

6

Liam came to, ears ringing, dust in his eyes. Blinking was agony – the dirt in the air kicked up by the explosion was like smashed glass poured into his eyes. For a moment he couldn't see a thing. Through tears he could just about make out some blurry shapes. He tried to blink again, shook his head as though that would bring the picture into focus, breathed, coughed, choking on fallout from the blast, then pushed himself up to a sitting position.

It took a moment for his head to clear. When it did, he remembered what had happened: Clint grabbing him round the neck, the sound of an explosion, everyone dropping to the ground, then everything had gone black.

Liam was on his feet. He was hot and sweat was dripping from his head. Wiping it away, he looked around. The remnants of his quarters were scattered, and above him the tent-like roof was shredded. His foot knocked against an army mess tin, a rectangular aluminium tin holding another similar tin inside it. A groan caught Liam's senses and he swept round to see Clint and Martin also stirring. Clint was on his feet first.

'Take it easy,' said Liam. 'You might be injured.'

'I'm not the one who's bleeding,' said Clint. 'You must've been hit by some of the stuff flying around the room from the explosion.'

Liam didn't know what Clint was on about. 'I'm fine,' he said.

Clint nodded to a shattered mirror hanging from a locker. 'Take a look at yourself. Either you're injured, or really bad at shaving.'

Liam glanced over and saw a face smeared with blood. He remembered wiping what he'd thought was sweat from his face. Looking at the red smear on the back of his hand he realized now that it hadn't been sweat at all.

'Didn't feel a thing,' he said.

'That'll be that thick skull of yours,' said Clint. 'You'll need looking at, though, even if you do feel fine. Injury could be hidden. Don't want you keeling over at random when we're on patrol.'

'We'll all get looked at,' said Liam, as they both reached down to check on Martin.

Outside, they could hear shouting, people running around. Then someone appeared in front of them.

'What have we got?' It was a medic and she was over to them in a moment, grab bag off her shoulder. 'You. Sit,' she said, pointing at Liam. 'And you,' she added, looking at Clint.

'I'm fine,' Liam said.

'I don't care if you think you can appear on an episode of *Strictly Come Dancing*,' the medic replied. 'You're bleeding. I need to check you over – all of you – and you're the most obviously injured. Here.' She handed him a field dressing as sat down on the edge of a bed. 'Press this against that cut on your forehead while I check this guy out.'

The medic bent down to where Martin still lay on the ground, covered with debris. She was only a shade smaller than Liam, with dark brown hair pulled back in an I-mean-business ponytail. Older, though, he thought, by at least five years. She walked with a sureness not only in her own skill, but in her physical capabilities; there was a lean look to her that said to anyone who knew the signs that she didn't just keep in shape – she was athlete-fit.

'What the hell happened?' asked Martin, pushing himself up from underneath all the kit that had been vomited over him by a locker now balancing across a bed. Liam almost felt sorry for him, considering how much time Martin had spent making sure that everything, from his socks to his beret, was neatly stored.

'Mortars,' said the medic. 'The ground outside camp is already being scoured for whoever launched them.'

'How did they get close enough?' asked Martin.

'There's always going to be some little sneaky place to hide up and wait for the right moment,' said the medic. 'And the Taliban are very good at finding them.'

'Yeah, and there's only so many checks on vehicles you can do,' said Liam. 'The Taliban are good at what they do. Very good. We wouldn't still be here if they weren't.'

Clint asked, 'What's the damage? Any serious injuries?'

The medic helped Martin to his feet then guided him over to sit on the bed beside Clint. 'Don't know yet,' she said, switching back to Liam to check him over properly. 'I just grabbed my bag of tricks and ran in here as I was so close.' She examined Liam's face, wiping it clean, then flushing the cuts with sterilized water, making sure he was carrying no other injuries before speaking again. 'I want you lot over to the medical centre immediately,' she stated.

Liam started to complain, but the stare the medic shot back stopped him dead.

'You're with 4 Rifles, right?'

Liam, Clint and Martin nodded.

'Then you're leaving camp in a couple of days. The last thing anyone wants is you lot charging off into the thick of it, then collapsing during your first patrol. You're all going to the medical centre.'

'I always thought angels of mercy would have a sweeter edge to them,' said Clint.

'You're seeing it,' said the medic. 'Now, all of you, up and out and fuck off over to the medical centre. Move!'

Liam was on a bed and getting itchy with impatience.

'I'm bloody well fine,' he said, looking at Martin. 'Why the hell am I still here? And, more to the point, why hang on to me and not you or Cowboy?'

'Perhaps that medic fancies you?' said Martin, grinning.

'Ha fuckity ha,' said Liam.

It wasn't just that he was impatient to get out, it was also that he was worried that some doctor was going to come along and say he couldn't head out with the rest of the battalion.

'I can't stay here,' he said. 'I can't. I need to get my stuff together. Replace anything that's damaged from the mortar attack.'

'You're in for twenty-four hours,' said Martin. 'That's it. And there's only twelve left to go.'

'What if I'm kept back?' asked Liam. 'What if I don't get to come out with you lot and end up stuck here in Bastion for the rest of the tour? Then what?'

'Doesn't sound so bad,' said Martin.

'Sounds fucking horrific!' said Liam. 'I'd go mental!' He slammed a fist down onto the bed.

'Someone's grumpy,' came a voice from behind Martin, and in walked the medic who'd come to them after the explosion had smashed apart their quarters. Her name was Nicky Harper, and this was her third tour. Liam had already realized that she didn't take any bullshit. It didn't stop him moaning.

'There's nothing wrong with me,' he said. 'I'm fine. It's just some cuts and bruises. Let me go. I've got stuff to do!'

The medic stood at the side of Liam's bed. 'So have I,' she said. 'And that includes making sure that the people I'm heading out into the badlands with are fit and well enough to be there in the first place and won't just walk off and get themselves blown up, shot or captured. Got me?'

Liam couldn't help but like Nicky. She didn't mess around, that was for sure. He'd also caught something in what she'd just said. 'You're coming with us?' he asked. It was the first he'd heard about it.

'Would I need your approval if I were?'

'That's not what I meant.'

'Good,' said Nicky. 'So do me a favour: shut up and let me do my job.'

She checked Liam over, but didn't give anything away. 'You were lucky,' she said eventually. 'All of you were. The mortar landed close, but most of the blast was directed elsewhere.'

'Am I OK?'

Nicky had a face on her a pro poker player would be proud of, thought Liam. 'Listen,' she said. 'You need to calm down a little, bin the impatience to get out of here and into what's out there. When I said you were lucky, I meant it. Some others didn't fare so well.'

Liam fell silent. Lying in his bed, his only occupying thought had been the fear of not heading out with the rest of 4 Rifles. He hadn't really given a thought to what else had been going on.

'What happened?' he asked.

'Four mortars were sent over the perimeter,' Nicky explained. 'One didn't detonate, so the bomb disposal lads had some fun with that. I tell you, they were almost excited.'

'And the other three?' asked Martin.

'You were one,' said Nicky. 'The other two caused considerably more damage.' She fell quiet, stood up. 'No one was killed,' she said. 'But a fair few were injured. And one lad is flying back home to sort out the mess that's been made of his leg. He's stable, but there's only so much that can be done out here. If they don't get him back ASAP, there's a chance he'll lose it.'

'Oh,' said Liam, because that was all he could say. He'd been too wrapped up in himself to give a moment's thought to anyone else.

'So like I said,' continued Nicky, 'don't be in too much of a rush. You were lucky. Deal with that first. Then, when it's time for you to leave, just do your job and do it well. It's not a race or a competition. The only thing that matters is to go back home alive.'

Nicky made to leave. As she neared the exit, Liam called after her, 'Harper?'

She turned.

'Cheers,' he said, and attempted a smile, but it fell from his face almost immediately, its brief appearance a moment of awkwardness he instantly wanted to forget.

Nicky nodded, then was gone.

'You're in there,' said Martin, leaning in, his voice the whisper of conspiracy.

'Don't be a twat,' said Liam. 'Didn't you see?'

'See what?'

Liam raised his left hand, waggled a finger. 'She's married,' he said.

For a moment, neither of them said anything. Then Martin shook his head. 'Poor bastard,' he said. 'Married to a bitch with a halo.'

Liam wasn't sure he agreed.

At last, Liam was free to go. And it was Nicky who delivered the news.

'Remember what I said: don't go being all impatient when it comes to soldiering. You know that anyway, but I'm just making sure.'

Liam swung off his bed as someone else walked in.

'Fit to go then, Scott? Not taking the easy route and staying at Bastion while the rest of us head out?' It was Corporal Cowell.

'Yes, Corporal,' said Liam, immediately wondering why he was getting a special visit. 'Harper here says I'm fine, right?'

Nicky nodded. 'He's good to go, Corporal.'

Liam caught Cowell glance at Nicky, then snap his eyes away almost like he didn't know where to look.

'You all right, Corporal?' asked Liam.

'Yes, absolutely, why wouldn't I be?'

'No reason.'

'I've just come to check that you've heard about the politician.'

Liam shook his head. 'No one's told me anything.'

'That's because I've only allowed Saunders in to visit you,' said Nicky. 'And he was under strict orders to worry you with nothing outside this room.'

Again, Liam caught Cowell glancing over at the medic.

'We're having a visit from someone important,' said Cowell. 'And they're turning up just before we're due to head out, which is all we need.'

'What does it matter?' asked Liam.

'It matters,' said Cowell, 'because everything needs to be perfect, or else we end up sending a politician back home thinking we can't hack it out here. That then gets fed back to the press, twisted, fucked around with, and everything goes tits up.'

'Spit and polish then,' said Liam.

'Beginning now,' said Cowell. 'As soon as you're out, start getting your shit together. And start off by having a shower and a shave. You look like a bag of bollocks.'

Without another word, not even a nod to Liam and Nicky, Cowell left.

'He's a bit weird, X-Factor,' said Liam. 'Can't work him out.'

'X-Factor?' said Nicky, then smiled. A rare sight, thought Liam. 'Oh, right, as in Simon Cowell!'

'That, and the fact he's also a prize bastard,' said Liam, then added, 'Did you see him, though? Why was he acting so weird?'

'There's a few like him left, I'm afraid,' said Nicky. 'Don't like the idea of women being out in the thick of it, and most definitely not out in theatre. See it as a man's job to be shot at.'

'So you are joining us?' Liam remembered Nicky mentioning it earlier but hadn't known if she was being serious or not.

'Lieutenant Steers has requested a female medic.'

'Why?'

'I'll be able to double up as a female searcher,' said Nicky. 'Just another way of building bridges and showing respect. Makes my life nice and interesting too.'

Liam thought about this and about what Nicky had said about Cowell. 'You know, there's probably a load of folk back home who'd agree with the corporal,' he said. 'You know, about women being in theatre.'

Nicky's head snapped up, eyes burning a hole in Liam's skull.

'And you? What do you think?'

Liam raised his hands in defence. 'Go crazy,' he said.

'Join in the fun! Anyway, I've seen you work. I want you out there, just in case.'

A flicker of another smile graced Nicky's mouth. 'You can always tell someone who's already been out in theatre,' she said. 'And someone who hasn't.'

Liam knew she was talking about Cowell.

'X-Factor will be fine,' he said. 'They wouldn't send him out if he was crap, would they?'

7

With the arrival of the politician imminent, Bastion went crazy. If it moved, it was pinned down and reinforced. If it didn't move, it was painted or polished. If you could drive it, then it was put in a nice neat line. Even the Apache helicopters. *Not that they need to be in any sort of line*, thought Liam, having seen them flying overhead every day since they'd arrived. *They're just cool, and they know it.*

After the mortar attack had gutted their quarters, Liam and the others had been moved to a new building. It looked no different from the last, not that Liam had expected it to. Bastion may have been huge, but it wouldn't be winning design awards anytime soon.

Liam was ironing all his clothes, hanging or folding them neatly away. They didn't have the locker space afforded them back in the UK, and had to make do with canvas wardrobes and shelves that collapsed for ease of transport. But that wasn't an excuse to let standards drop, or at least that was what they'd been told.

'I thought I'd left all this shit behind when I finished my Phase 2,' said Martin, buffing his boots to a blinding sheen. 'What use is a shiny boot out here? Does anyone really care?'

'Is there a problem?'

Liam didn't need to turn to see who it was: Corporal Cowell.

'No, Corporal,' Martin replied, his hand paused above his boots.

'Don't let my interruption stop you, Saunders,' said Cowell. 'And what was it you were saying about Phase 2?'

'That it was the best time of his whole life,' said Clint, clearly joining in to support Martin. 'We all feel the same, don't we, lads?'

Everyone offered a brief acknowledgement, but Cowell was obviously not in the mood. 'You trying to be a funny man?' he asked, sidling up now to Clint. 'Bit of a comedian, are we?'

Liam had stopped ironing. Whatever was going to happen next was sure to be a whole lot more interesting. He'd already clocked that Cowell and Clint didn't see eye-to-eye. Though he was surprised to see them both so open about it.

'No, Corporal,' said Clint. 'Being in the army is a very serious business indeed.'

Liam caught the hint of sarcasm, but Clint's face was stony and gave nothing away to Cowell.

'That's good then,' said Cowell, eyeing Clint hard, 'because if I can't trust you sad fucks to get even the basics right, to keep a place and yourselves clean, rather than turn everything into a shit tip, how do you think I'm going to feel?'

No one said anything.

Cowell leaned forward, his nose only millimetres away from Clint's chin. 'I asked how you think I'd feel?' he said. 'And it is not a rhetorical question. I want an answer.'

Clint eventually said, 'It's all in the detail, Corporal.'

'Too fucking right it is!' Cowell spat back, the words out of him quicker than poison. 'So how's about we stop the complaining and belly-aching and give it some, eh?'

Footsteps approached and Miller, with a smirk on his face, appeared behind Cowell.

'Everything spick and span, lads?'

'All good,' Corporal Cowell replied.

Miller nodded. 'Excellent,' he said. 'Can't show a

politician grubby soldiers and muddy grenades now, can we? Might get the impression we don't know how to look after ourselves.'

Miller left. Cowell grinned.

'Once you've finished whatever the fuck it is you're doing, I want the floor matting up and the gravel underneath raked flat. Uneven floors are dangerous. And they look like crap.'

Liam couldn't believe what he was hearing. 'You want us to rake the floor?'

'I'm sorry, is there an echo in here?'

Liam said nothing more.

'Didn't think so,' said Cowell. 'See you later, lads, eh? Have fun.' And he was gone.

'They'll have us polishing our fucking rounds next,' said Ade. 'Jobsworth bastards.'

'You mean you've not done yours yet?' asked Clint. 'Shame on you, Sunter.'

'It's their job,' said Liam. 'It's like Cowboy said, it's all in the detail.'

Ade snorted. 'And what are you, Scott, X-Factor's pet?'

Liam knew arguing with Ade was pointless, so he went back to his ironing.

It was early afternoon when the politician eventually

arrived and was given the official guided tour – the one that didn't include the shit pits and focused much more on the amazing resources, the state-of-the-art hospital, and the row upon row of shiny bits of hard-looking metal. Liam joined the rest of 4 Rifles, all standing at ease, out in front of some neatly placed helicopters and other impressive motorized transport.

Grey clouds were high in the sky, doing little to combat the raging heat from the sun, and Liam hoped that whatever the politician was going to say, it would be quick, to the point, and over in a few minutes, so they could all get back to sorting their kit and prepping themselves mentally as well as physically. Preferably in the shade.

The politician, a woman called Hilary Barton, stood behind a microphone in front of the troops. She was dressed in sand-coloured clothing, observed Liam, in some poor attempt to combat the heat, look smart, and to try and fit in. With her were the top brass of Camp Bastion and some not-inconspicuously-dressed bodyguards. Liam had heard that she was part of the Cabinet and had been sent over by the Prime Minister on a morale-boosting mission, though he was pretty sure that anything she did or said would make little if any difference to his morale. He got that from his mates, from the folk he'd be living with in the dust and grime of some

Afghan compound, people he could trust to back him up in a firefight. And from the reliability of the weapons at his disposal. If he couldn't depend on any of that, he might as well give up now.

As Hilary Barton began to speak, Liam tuned out. He couldn't quite hear her anyway, and he wasn't overly bothered about what she was here to say. Instead, he spent a few minutes running over a few things in his mind: weapons drills, how to sort out a casualty, stripping and cleaning his SA80, how to handle a Gimpy . . .

'. . . role is no longer a case of taking the fight to the Taliban. We are here to work with the locals and to eventually hand over security to the Afghan National Army.'

Liam's ears pricked up. Perhaps what she was saying was relevant after all. He wouldn't put money on it, though.

'Courageous Restraint,' continued the politician, 'was a term coined some time ago and perhaps misinterpreted by some. But the motivation behind it, the reasoning, is still something we should all think about.'

She paused, Liam assumed to add drama to what she was saying. What he *didn't* like was that she sounded like she was about to start telling them about the ROE – Rules of Engagement. And that just didn't seem right coming from a glorified office clerk. That stuff was down to generals, the ones running the operation who knew exactly what was going on. Not some vote-grabber without a clue about anything.

Barton spoke again, this time with renewed purpose, her voice pitched at a well-practised serious tone. 'We must not be seen as a force looking for war, but instead looking for peace. We must not be judged by our willingness to open fire, but instead by our courage in holding *off* the trigger, and engaging in conversation.'

Another pause. She was being clever, thought Liam. Without directly mentioning the ROE she was getting away with sounding like she was here just to give them all something to think about. It was dangerous ground. Soldiers didn't like being told what to do by politicians, period, even if it was dressed up all fancy.

Barton leaned forward, emphasizing her words with carefully rehearsed hand gestures. 'We are here to help the Afghan people regain their lands, their lives, from the Taliban, and to do that we must show them that the only way forward is the path of tolerance, understanding and compromise. Then shall we all have peace.'

The politician went on some more, but Liam was no longer listening. He was trying to compute what she'd just said. Because, to his mind, and remembering everything he'd experienced during his last tour, the concept of Courageous Restraint, however morally justified, sounded like complete and total bollocks.

Not being able to fire back scared him shitless.

8

A while later, waiting to gather for a final get-together before heading out, Liam was sitting staring at his kit, all packed and ready to go. He was tempted to strip his weapon again to keep himself occupied, but resisted.

'You're quiet,' said Clint.

'Mmm,' said Liam.

'And talkative.'

Liam apologized. 'It's what that woman was on about,' he said. 'Courageous Restraint sounds mental.'

'She wasn't advocating it,' said Clint. 'Just using it to support her views. Anyway, Courageous Restraint was binned back when that US general left theatre.'

Liam stayed quiet.

'You've read Card Alpha. That's all you need to worry about.'

Card Alpha was the name given to the strict Rules of Engagement – ROE – set out by the British Army. It didn't look anything special, just a small, laminated, yellow card that every soldier carried with them. But the weight of power it held was that of life and death, literally.

'Still,' said Liam, 'she seemed pretty clear on what she thought about what we should be doing.'

'That's her job,' said Clint, and he tapped a finger on Liam's forehead. 'You just keep up here the six-step targeting process, right? Go through that checklist every time something is about to kick off and you'll know if you're morally and legally allowed to engage an enemy.'

'I know we have the right to self-defence,' said Liam. 'But all that stuff about holding off the trigger and having a chat? She's having a laugh, right?'

'It's her job to say the right thing to whoever is, or may be, listening,' said Clint, 'That's all she really said.'

'How the hell is going over to shake the hand of someone emptying an AK at me going to help?' Liam asked. He was getting agitated now. Not at Clint, but at what the politician had said. He couldn't understand it.

'It's about protecting lives,' said Clint, 'particularly civilian ones. This is no longer a war, mate. We're handing over to the ANA. Soon we'll be gone and they'll be alone to face what's left. What they need is the locals on their side, rather than on the Taliban's. That's what it's about.'

'You believe that?'

Clint shrugged. 'I have to. We all have to.' He checked his watch. 'Come on. Time to go listen to Miller and Cowell brief us again on the details of our new hotel. I hope it has a swimming pool. In this heat, it's going to be no holiday without one.'

A few minutes later, Liam and Clint sat down with Martin, Ade, Rob and the rest of the multiple he would be stationed with. Lieutenant Steers took the stand, with Miller, Cowell and the other NCOs alongside. Everyone knew the lieutenant would be running the show. And with the support of NCOs like Miller, Liam had some confidence that their leadership was strong.

'Right, I'll get straight to the point,' said the lieutenant. 'In a little under an hour you will all be saying goodbye to this holiday camp and heading off to do the job you get paid for. Like all of you, I'm keen to get out there and get on with it.'

Everyone nodded and Liam heard a few murmurs of 'Too right, sir,' and 'About bloody time'.

The lieutenant was a tall man, athletically built, with cropped dark hair and serious eyes. Liam knew, as they all did, that he was in the presence of an excellent leader.

This was no short-term officer looking for a bit of experience before heading off into civvy-street. This was a man here for the duration, a career soldier to his very core.

'I don't need to stand here and tell you what you need to do, so I won't,' continued the lieutenant. 'You've already been told, by Major Varley, by Miller and the rest, and by me. However, I for one would prefer it if you didn't set off out of Bastion in an hour leaving shit behind for someone else to sort out. Understood?'

There was another murmur of agreement. Liam knew what Lieutenant Steers was getting at. Once out of Camp Bastion, they'd be as good as cut off from the outside world. No mobiles. Post would be sporadic at best. They would also be living under the constant threat of injury and death. And that meant sorting out goodbyes and death letters, just like Major Varley had ordered. Being reminded again was, Liam knew, just the army way – keep telling you until it becomes instinct. Liam had written his during his last tour and his parents would get it in the event of his death. It had been a tough thing to write for numerous reasons, but he'd got it done and that was that. However, he couldn't help wondering how it was for Clint. Having a family at home, two young kids? That was a totally different situation, and if he was honest he wasn't quite sure how he'd deal with it if he were in the same position. He had no frame of reference, not with his own family the way it was – a dad who cared more for the contents of a bottle than for his son and a mum too timid to stand up to him.

The lieutenant allowed his eyes to cast a glare around the men in front of him. Somehow he managed to catch the eye of each and every soldier. It wasn't a threatening glare, but one that said, quite simply: *You will do your best – I fully expect it.* Liam also noticed clear respect between the lieutenant and Miller and that was reassuring. Despite this, though, he was still thinking about what the politician had said. It had unnerved him. He wondered if the lieutenant was now going to back her up and tell them that they had to think twice about firing back if the Taliban attacked.

The lieutenant spoke once more. 'We'll be patrolling villages,' he said, 'building and improving relations with the locals, providing medical checks, visible security, with the aim of handing security over to the ANA. We shall, as Major Varley stated, lead by example. That is our mission statement. That is what we are here to do. Trust me when I say we shall do it well. Any questions?'

Liam's hand was up before he could stop himself.

It was Corporal Cowell who answered, not Steers. 'Yes, what is it, Scott?'

'It's just about what that politician said,' said Liam. 'What happens when we get attacked? What rules are we following?'

Liam knew he sounded pissed off. He couldn't help it. They were heading out into dangerous territory and there were people out there waiting to kill them.

'It's like Lieutenant Steers just said,' answered Cowell, backing up his commanding officer. 'We're going to be leading by example. We can't go off on one and blast the shit out of every grassy knoll hiding some Tally fucker taking a pot shot. That's not going to win anyone a medal.'

Was that a dig? thought Liam. Was Cowell suggesting he was out here for glory?

'That's not what I'm saying,' said Liam, but Cowell shut him down.

'It's not fucking Rorke's Drift or the Charge of the Light Brigade. You all know Card Alpha. And you all – instinctively, I bloody well hope – know the six-step targeting process, right?'

'Yes, Corporal,' said Liam.

'Well, while we're here then, Scott, how's about you run through it for us, just to make sure?'

Bastard, thought Liam.

'On your feet, Scott.'

Liam stood. 'You want all six?'

Cowell nodded and Liam noticed a faint grin.

'One, establish ROE – Rules of Engagement. Two, PID – positively identify target. Three, all reasonable steps taken to minimize collateral damage.'

'What do you mean by that?' asked Cowell.

Fucking bastard, thought Liam. 'Correct weapon system for situation, Corporal,' he said. 'Four, battle damage assessment to minimize Taliban propaganda. Five, clearance – can I, should I, must I?'

'And six?' asked Cowell.

'Engage,' said Liam, and sat down. Sounding out the six steps had taken him straight back to his days of training, always having to prove you knew what you were doing, the assumption always seeming to be that you knew fuck all.

'Thank you, Scott,' said Cowell. 'You've answered your own question. Right?'

Liam caught a glance shoot between Sergeant Miller and Lieutenant Steers. It was the lieutenant who stepped in.

'Let me assure each and every one of you here, your safety is paramount.' The expression on the man's face was as hard as granite. He meant every word and his commitment to the men in front of him was unshakeable. 'Card Alpha is there to protect you. You all know it inside out. And if anyone is stupid enough to decide to come along and have a go at us, and those six points Scott sounded out are ticked off . . .' Lieutenant Steers fell silent, his face stern.

Then Miller stood up and a cold and rarely seen hard grin flickered.

'Fuck 'em,' he said.

9

Liam was strapped into the back of a Chinook, one of the huge twin-rotor helicopters used to ferry around everything from soldiers and supplies to vehicles and casualties. With afternoon drawing on, the day seemed even darker now that they were away from Bastion. As Patrol Base 1 – PB1 – was situated in a very remote part of the Yakchal Valley, they were flying in. Driving there would have taken considerably longer, with the risk of drawing attention from any Taliban along the way.

Liam's Personal Role Radio – PRR – was switched off for the flight, not that it would have made any difference. The only people who could hear anything were the flight crew, and they were using their own separate communication system.

The weather had taken a turn for the worse. It had been pretty much non-stop sun since they'd arrived, but now a wind was getting up and it had been touch and go as to whether they would be delayed. Everyone had been relieved when they'd got the go-ahead to set off. Despite Bastion's comforts, everyone wanted to get on with the job in hand. Waiting only prolonged the agony of nervous anticipation at what was waiting for them.

Liam had, from the moment he'd first seen a Chinook up close, been in bewildered awe of not just the machines themselves, but the pilots keeping them in the air. The choppers seemed almost to disobey all the laws of gravity, as well as sense and logic. Soldiers affectionately called them 'cows', a term which Liam thought was a bit unfair, as although they did look ungainly on the ground, when in the air they had a real presence to them, the kind of craft that owned the sky. A part of him envied pilots – flying helicopters was possibly the coolest job on the planet. That something so big, ugly and cumbersome could be flown with such accuracy and grace astonished him. The sight of them coming in to land, or just buzzing through the air like fat, drunken wasps, always gave him a boost of confidence. Liam realized this probably had a lot to do with the fact that one had come to his rescue during his last tour. He had been lost in the field and carrying an injured mate with the Taliban closing in. He had used every last bit of energy he had left to leg it to the open rear door of the Chinook that had come to their rescue. Sergeant Reynolds had been in the back, yelling at them to get a move on, while at the same time holding the Taliban back with a relentless spray of rounds from the Gimpy fixed in the tail.

With the signal sent round that they were soon to come in to land, and with the vivid memory of that day making him smile, Liam looked up to glance around at everyone else in the back of the Chinook with him. Not counting the crew of the Chinook, he was racing over the Afghanistan desert with eleven others, all of them heavily armed and ready to go. He had to admit that all crammed together they looked like a ferocious fighting force.

The multiple comprised Lieutenant Steers, supported by Sergeant Miller, Corporal Cowell and Lance Corporal Clark, with Liam and the rest of the lads – eight of them in total, including himself – making up the rest. Nicky was an addition, bringing their number to a lucky thirteen. Across to Liam's left, furthest from the rear door, she looked relaxed and calm.

Liam knew this was a big moment. Once they landed and stepped out of the helicopter, onto the Helicopter Landing Site – HLS – their whole lives changed. Life in Bastion was relatively safe. Out here, though, every day brought with it the risk of serious injury or death.

Martin was directly opposite. Liam noticed the Chinook dipping now, clearly heading in to land. He stared across at Martin, who was fiddling with his lucky rugby ball keyring, caught his eye, nodded and smiled. Martin just stared back. Unable to speak or even shout over the sound of the engines and the rotor blades, Liam mouthed, 'You'll be fine,' and gave a thumbs-up. Martin eventually responded with a nervous smile and a return thumbs-up.

Liam saw a shard of light grow across the inside of the cabin as the rear door of the Chinook lowered to allow everyone to exit quickly. This was a precautionary measure – get it done now so that their exit could be smooth and quick and allow the helicopter to leave ASAP. On the ground the Chinook was an easy target.

Out through the door, Liam caught his first glance of where he was going to be living. It was a bleak landscape of scrub and desert and rock, and all around, staring down, were mountains: huge rocky figures silently watching another fight at their feet. Patrol Base 1 itself was a walled compound, and more substantially built than Liam was expecting. Usually, compounds were mud-walled, but this was brick, as far as he could tell, reinforced by piles of sandbags. As for what was inside, he couldn't yet tell. Running alongside it was a wide road.

Liam rested his head back, closed his eyes, and prepared himself for what was to come.

And it was then – as the Chinook touched down on the HLS near Patrol Base 1 – that the RPG hit . . .

The flash of the blast blinded Liam for a moment and the aircraft bucked to one side, tipping him forward. The grenade had, he realized, smashed into the outside of the helicopter, though by some stroke of luck it had failed to pierce the fuselage and cause a bloodbath. But he knew with utter certainty that the Taliban were sure to follow up with another hit.

Seconds later, Liam was on his feet, rifle at the ready, half dragging, half carrying his kit, and racing out of the back of the Chinook. Hard ground met him, a mix of baked soil, sand and rock. He switched on his PRR. They had all been issued with the small transmitter-receiver radio, which allowed them to communicate over short distances, even through buildings and walls. Soldiers still learned all the usual shouted orders and hand signals, but the PRR had seriously upped their combat effectiveness in theatre.

Wind whipped around him, coming from the blades of the crippled Chinook and a blast that howled its way out of distant mountain passes. Dirt and dust swirled through the air. Patrol Base 1 was little more than two hundred metres away, but Liam had a feeling that he wouldn't be getting there without a fight. Then he spotted the telltale trail of another RPG heading towards them. Instinct took over and he dropped to the ground, covering his head as the missile hammered into the back of the helicopter and tore it apart. The heat of the explosion sucked the air dry, pulling it from his lungs.

Liam felt something zip past and then thump into the ground. That he was able to feel it was enough – a clear indication that whatever it was had landed within a metre of him. It was time to get a move on.

When he looked up, Liam saw that it wasn't a round of enemy fire – it was a section of the Chinook's fuselage, at least a metre in diameter. Its ragged edges were sharp and twisted and Liam knew that if he had dropped to the ground just a step earlier, it would have cut him in two. A messy way to go, but probably quick.

Liam heard the snap and crack of rounds overhead. Experience took over and he quickly identified where the direction of fire was coming from. He called it out over the PRR.

'Right! Three hundred! Ten o'clock!'

Three short commands, but enough to help, telling everyone not just where the fire was coming from, but also the range.

When the lads followed his directions, Liam's confidence leaped. He wasn't just a grunt, he was a soldier and they respected him enough to listen to him and his experience. At the same time he was up on one knee, rifle into his shoulder, and staring down the LDS attached to his SA80, returning fire. The ROE was a given – a firefight was on.

As he joined in and returned fire, Liam caught the sound of a large round being fired close by. Turning, he spotted another soldier, but the weapon he was holding was no ordinary SA80.

In his late twenties, with hair blond enough to make Flash Gordon envious, sharp cheekbones, and his height hitting six foot two, Neil Carter looked like he'd stepped out of an advert in *GQ*. So much so, in fact, that it had become his nickname.

Neil's weapon was the L115A3 rifle. Firing an 8.59mm round, it had improved range over its predecessor, the L96. It came with state-of-the-art telescopic day-and-night all-weather sights, and was capable of a first-round hit at 600 metres, its range extending up to 1100 metres. It was one serious weapon.

Calmly, Neil took his shots, making sure each one counted. Liam could see their effect through his own sights. He hadn't yet tried out the L11, and he didn't mind admitting that he was itching to get his mitts on the Sharpshooter as well, but that was in the hands of Lance Corporal Clark, who as well as being an NCO, was an excellent shot. And that meant he wouldn't be getting a look in.

A shout came in over the PRR. 'Scott!'

While Neil fired another deadly round, Liam turned to see Miller signalling to him from about fifteen metres away.

'Right! Two-fifty! One o'clock!'

That meant rounds were coming in from another direction. This wasn't just a random attack, it was well planned and seeming increasingly like an ambush.

Liam hammered a few more rounds into where he had identified incoming fire, changed magazines, then stared hard at where Miller was telling him to look. Lieutenant Steers was directing other soldiers to find cover and return fire. After the relative calm of Camp Bastion the shock of the firefight was almost overwhelming. But as always, Liam's training just took over. It was instinctive. It had to be. There was no time during a contact to ponder on the meaning of life, because as soon as you did, there was a chance a round would thump home and end it in a smashing of bone and ripping of flesh.

He spotted a knot of bush and scrub clambering up and around a long section of crumbling mud wall. Then muzzle flash. Then another. Liam had no idea how many Taliban were hiding there, but that didn't matter. All that mattered was stopping them.

Liam opened fire. At this range, with the target at least a hundred metres away, fully auto was a waste of rounds. You only ever used that if things had gone seriously to shit and all other options were dead. Instead, Liam peppered the place as rapidly as he could with accurate fire, the SA80 coming into its own as a weapon with a worldwide reputation for unequalled accuracy. He changed his magazine again in one smooth motion, hardly missing a beat.

Heavy fire was coming from the compound now – the lads already at the patrol base were up at the walls and pummelling the surrounding area with a deadly rate of firepower. Liam saw Clint giving it some with his own rifle. He hadn't yet seen Martin but was sure he was being kept busy too. It was one hell of a way to start off a tour.

The ground around Liam was peppered with rounds coming in thick and fast. Some were tracers, zipping a bright red line through the air. Flaming wreckage from the ruined Chinook covered the area. It was apocalyptic, a bleak landscape of flame and violence.

Liam checked again for direction of fire, then heard another shout over the radio. Miller again. He turned.

Miller was jabbing a finger behind Liam. Despite the effectiveness of the PRR, a physical order was still advisable. It was also reassuring to see someone in control, not to just hear them.

Liam turned and saw one of the large boxes of supplies they'd brought with them. And he was the closest.

Miller yelled across the radio to Clint and any other soldiers close enough to help, 'Give Scott covering fire! Now!'

If the sound of rifle fire had been loud before, it was deafening now. And with his mates putting down a wall of hot metal on anyone idiotic enough to get in the way, Liam was on his feet, racing hard for the supplies, zigzagging all the way to make himself a difficult target, wondering what the hell Miller had in mind.

Unclipping the webbing that held the supplies securely together, Liam soon found out.

Ripping open a box, he pulled out a metal tube about a metre long. It was a light anti-structures missile, or LASM for short. The 66mm unguided extendable rocket launcher carried a kilo of explosives. After piercing through a target the high-explosive warhead would detonate. Liam had used the weapon more than once during his last tour. And now he picked it up and had it sighted on the target in a heartbeat.

Liam breathed out, eyes focused down the pop-up sight of the launcher. Then he pressed the black switch on top of the green tube.

The rocket leaped out, tracing a faint white trail through the air. Then it crashed into the wall, exploding a moment later on the other side, right where the Taliban were laid up and firing from.

The explosion ripped the area to pieces, chucking dirt and stone and anything else in its way high into the air. It was impossible to tell at this distance, but Liam knew that amongst the debris were the remains of whoever had been firing at them.

The firing stopped. Liam dropped the now empty and useless tube, grabbed another and ran forward.

More rounds came in, this time from another direction. Still zigzagging, he dropped down beside Clint. Rob was with him – for once without his iPod on – along with a soldier with bright red hair whose name was Tim Harding. Of everyone Liam had met, Harding was the quietest, hardly ever saying a word.

'Nice welcome we get, isn't it?' said Clint. 'Where's the warm handshake, mug of tea and biscuit?'

Rob switched mags, fired. 'I could murder a fucking brew,' he said, agreeing with Clint. 'And a Rich Tea.'

One thing Liam had quickly become used to was squaddie humour. Dry and dark, it helped them all cope with extreme danger and the threat of death. It wasn't uncommon to even hear laughter during a firefight, albeit it grim and cold.

'Fuckers were waiting for us,' continued Rob, talking between shots. 'Like they knew we were coming.'

'Bollocks,' said Liam, changing his own mag. 'How could they?'

'Think about it,' said Rob. 'The only ones who would've known we were on our way were the lads in the compound. We don't go broadcasting our every movement, not unless we actually want to get shot to pieces.'

Liam raised his rifle and, with Sergeant Miller now controlling return of fire from his troops, joined in with Clint. He couldn't help but think about what Rob had suggested, though, and he didn't like it. The implication – that someone on the inside of the compound had given away their imminent arrival – was terrifying.

'Are you saying someone told them?'

'All I know,' said Rob, 'is that we arrived into a whole world of shit and someone knew enough about where we were, and when we'd arrive, to lay it all on for us.'

Liam heard Corporal Cowell shouting orders, and he wasn't exactly coming across as someone who'd never been in combat before. Perhaps he'd misjudged him? he thought. It was reassuring. The bloke might not be such a total arsehole after all.

Whatever peace had rested on the place before they'd arrived had now been duly shattered. But that, thought Liam, was the fault of the daft fuck who had decided to take a pot shot at them with an RPG. He wondered at the sense of it really, now that, with their arrival, there were twice as many well-trained soldiers to deal with.

Miller dropped in next to Liam, Clint, Rob and Tim. 'Eastwood, Harding, Hammond – you're with me,' he said. 'The lads in the compound have them pinned down. We're moving along their left flank to cut them off. Scott?'

'Boss?' Liam answered.

Miller pointed back up at the charred remains of the helicopter. 'Harper's up there dealing with injuries. The pilots got hammered. Two casualties. She needs assistance and you're it as you're closest. Clark will be following. We need them stabilized and taken to PB One, ASAP. Move!'

Liam nodded, caught Clint's eye, then sprinted back to the Chinook, legs hammering like engine pistons. Now acclimatized to the Afghan heat, the sprint didn't bother him one bit.

Behind the Chinook he found Nicky and the two wounded pilots.

'Hold this,' Nicky shouted over the noise of the fire-fight, handing him a drip. It was attached to one of the pilots. 'Talk to him. He's all right, but I've the other one to check over again.'

Liam took the drip, dropped down at the pilot's side. The man was clearly in pain, every breath causing him to wince – morphine could only do so much. His head was bandaged and bleeding, and the rest of him was dotted with field dressings gradually turning a pinky red. Dust and dirt had mixed with the blood, staining it a dirty, grubby brown. Infection could be as much a killer in war as the actual wound.

'Miller's called in for air support,' said Nicky, now working with another casualty. 'We need to extract all casualties to PB One immediately. I've radioed in for medevac. They'll come in once everything has calmed down.' She crawled over to another figure lying in the shadow of the Chinook.

As Liam chatted to the pilot, working at keeping him awake and his mind off his injuries, a series of sharp, violent explosions tore his voice from him and he leaned forward over the pilot, using his body to protect him from any fallout. 'What the fuck was that?'

The pilot tried to speak, but pain stabbed his

words. At last he said, 'Sounds like . . . Hellfires.'

Liam almost felt sorry for anyone on the receiving end of such a weapon. There was simply no escape.

'And that means,' said the pilot, toughing it out against the pain to keep talking, 'the Apache helicopter brigade have come to join in the fun.'

Another barrage followed, then silence. And right at the edge of it, the faint throb of rotor blades, drawing closer.

'See?' said the pilot, and Liam saw them through the dust, far enough away not to be at risk of a rocket attack, but close enough to cause horrifying mayhem. Faint puffs of smoke burst from the helicopter silhouettes.

'That'll be CRV7 rockets now,' said the pilot as the rockets streaked the sky towards their target. He tried to sit up to get a better look, but gave up barely a second into trying.

'Effective?' asked Liam.

'They'll be armed with flechette warheads,' said the pilot, closing his eyes in pain. 'Each one has eighty tungsten darts, all capable of piercing two-inch-thick armour plating. If there's anything left that's alive, it won't be for much longer.' He opened his eyes and looked up at Liam with a best attempt at a grin, then said, 'Gleaming!'

Now that was a word Liam loved to hear. 'Gleaming'

was the ultimate seal of approval from a soldier. So, clearly, whatever the Apaches were about to do, it was going to be seriously effective.

Liam didn't see what happened next, his view blocked by the Chinook. There was no explosion, just the faint sound of dirt and grit being hit hard by what the pilot had just described.

'It'll be over now,' said the pilot. 'Trust me.'

Although the sense of urgency and danger had receded, for the next half an hour or so Liam heard sporadic bursts of gunfire. He guessed this was little more than the others clearing through where the Taliban had been hiding out.

Corporal Cowell appeared. Nicky looked up. With Cowell were four other lads from the multiple.

'On your order, Harper, covering fire will hammer what's left of those Tally bastards attacking us, and you and the boys here get the wounded to PB One. Understood?'

'Corporal.' Nicky nodded, then said, 'Let's do this now. We're good to go.'

The lads with Cowell grabbed the casualties. Cowell called across the PRR and a rapid rate of fire was laid down. Anyone stupid enough to pop their head up for a look-see now would get it shot off. Then the casualties were off, the lads carrying them racing across open ground to Patrol Base 1, their only cover the massive and deadly amount of live rounds being pummelled into the Taliban positions.

Clint's voice came over the PRR. 'Saunders is hit!' The words rang hard, crystal clear, deafening. 'We need to extract to PB One! Immediately!'

10

Liam looked up, but before he could speak another voice came over the radio: it was Steers.

'Eastwood, can you make PB One with Saunders?'

'Sir!'

No hesitation. Not a hint of it. Liam knew right then that Clint was exactly the kind of soldier he wanted alongside him. He was professional, knew exactly what he was doing, and got the job done, period.

'On my order, everyone will provide covering fire. Cowell?'

Cowell came back with, 'Sir?'

'Once Eastwood is at PB One, we extract the rest of the team. Covering fire will be provided from the compound.'

Cowell acknowledged the order. Liam didn't want to think about Saunders. Couldn't. He still had to fight his own way back to the PB and stay alive.

On Steers's order, the world erupted again with a hail of metal. Liam saw Clint jump up, Martin across his shoulders in a fireman's carry. He was racing hard, sprinting to Patrol Base 1. Hell, he was quick . . .

'The rest of you – MOVE!' Steers's voice was as commanding over the PRR as it was in real life.

Liam was up and he was off, drawing on energy reserves only a squaddie would know about.

The compound was alive with the excitement of the firefight. Liam raced through the doors and looked around for Clint. Soldiers were everywhere.

'Scott! Up there! Now!'

It was Miller, pointing to the walls. Liam pushed aside his worry for Martin and headed off.

Up top, he had a better view of the compound. It was much bigger than the compounds he'd stayed in before. Not only that, it housed considerably more men. During his last tour, it had been just one multiple at a patrol base. Here, though, a number of multiples were stationed together, as the British forces had reduced the number of patrol bases considerably.

Liam ignored his observations and got down to laying down some fire. He changed another magazine, then zipped the rounds into where the few remaining Taliban were hiding. He was fully focused. All that mattered was being a soldier, standing side by side with his mates, and taking the fight back good and hard against those who'd brought it to their door.

'Stop!'

It was the lieutenant's voice and on his command everyone in the compound eased off their triggers.

An eerie silence cascaded into the space where the rattle and clatter of gunfire had lived. It was so acutely different that for a second Liam, ears ringing from the rounds, wondered if he could actually hear the silence.

Movement behind him. The lieutenant was calling soldiers over, putting a group together to go check on the damage. They'd be covered by everyone else in the compound. It had to be done now, and quickly. If there was the chance of a prisoner, this was the best time to go hunting. It was also a good idea to make sure no one went running back to the Taliban with further news. Or to bring back immediate reinforcements.

Weapon made safe, sweat pouring from him now, and the exertion of the firefight quickly ripping itself through his every fibre, Liam went and found Clint, who was crouched on the ground and leaning against a wall. He was covered in dust, his clothing patched with sweat, but darker stains lay there too: blood.

'What's happened? Where is he? Where's Mascot?'

'We think he got cut off from the rest of us when we bugged out of the Chinook,' said Clint, clearly using all the energy he had left to keep his voice steady and his emotions in check. 'Ran the wrong way or something. We don't know. His body—'

Liam caught the word, threw it back fast-ball quick. 'What do you mean, his body? He was shot, right? Wounded! What's happened?'

Clint took a deep breath. Liam could see now that he was holding back tears. And that was enough. He didn't need to hear any more. He knew. But still the words came, slow and horrid and wrong.

'We found him out on his own,' Clint said. 'Lying face down in a shallow scrape, covering himself, like we all did, when the second RPG hit.'

Liam didn't want to hear it. Not again. Not Martin. Was he destined to lose close friends for the rest of his life? Was he a jinx? Bad luck for others?

'A stray round must've got him,' said Clint. 'Somehow, it—' His voice broke. 'I . . . we did what we could, Liam, but he was gone by the time we got to the compound.'

The twisted, raw emotions of the moment ripped out of Liam in a roar. He grabbed Clint, heaved him up against a wall. 'Why weren't you with him? Why wasn't someone with him? He was new! How the fuck could this happen?'

Clint faced Liam down. 'It's no one's fault, Scott,' he

said, voice measured, but cracking. 'It could've just as easily been you or me.'

'Bollocks, it could!' Liam spat back. 'Someone should've been with him! It should've been me or you! He was counting on us, Cowboy, and we fucking well failed him!'

'You want to punch me, go ahead, if it'll make you feel better,' said Clint.

Liam wanted to. He wanted to lash out and kick the living shit out of everything in sight, rip down walls, tear doors to splinters. But it would make no difference at all.

'He's gone, mate,' said Clint. 'There's nothing we can do.'

Liam tried to struggle, but his fight had evaporated. 'I was gonna look out for him,' he said. 'After we got hit, I . . . but . . .' His voice died as a volley of images of Martin filled his mind. He hadn't known him long, but the loss was an earthquake and it had completely destabilized him. 'It can't be true,' he said at last, finding his strength again, standing to talk to Clint. 'You're sure it's him? Absolutely sure?'

He then saw Rob walk past and remembered what he'd said.

'Someone tipped them off . . .' Liam's voice was quiet, a whisper almost.

Clint leaned in. 'You what?'

'They knew we were coming.'

'They couldn't have done,' said Clint. 'We just turned up at the wrong time. What you're suggesting is, well, it's just not right. And neither is it possible.'

'I'm not suggesting anything,' said Liam. 'I'm just saying we need to keep an eye out, that's all, just in case.'

Clint shook his head. 'What have you heard? Who told you this?'

Liam said nothing more about it, and changed the subject back to Martin. 'We'll need to sort his kit out,' he said. 'I did it for Cam.'

'We can do it together,' Clint replied, voice calm, reassuring. 'If that's OK with you? We both knew him.'

'He didn't even get a chance to fight back,' Liam muttered, the fight gone from his voice, but not from the sentiment. 'The bastards . . .'

Clint rested a hand on Liam's shoulder, his eyes dark and fierce. 'Scott, mate, that's our job, right?'

Cowell's voice came over the PRR. The medevac had arrived and Liam could hear the distinct throb of another Chinook coming in to land next to its dead sister.

'Not exactly the Hilton, is it?'

Clint was with Liam, carrying their kit across the

compound like two well-trained pack horses. Evening was drawing in. It wasn't dark yet, but the sun was low and bleeding across the sky like it too had been wounded in the fight. Soldiers milled everywhere.

The multiple that Liam's had replaced at Patrol Base 1 were on their way back to Camp Bastion with the casualties. The last time Liam had been in Afghanistan, the checkpoints he'd manned up in Helmand had all been absolute hell holes. They'd even called one Room 101, it had been such a total nightmare. Cut off and falling apart, the only way to improve it would've been to flatten it with a few well-aimed JDAMs, huge unguided gravity bombs with massive destructive power. It certainly couldn't have been any worse. Or at least that was what Liam had thought until thirty seconds ago.

'Have we just walked onto the set of a movie about the early days of the Foreign Legion?' he asked, trying to take it all in.

'Even those nutjobs wouldn't put up with this,' said Clint. 'It's an old police station. Not that you can tell that now, thanks to all the HESCOs surrounding it.'

HESCO was the name given to the huge multi-cellular wall units, filled with whatever material was available to hand – in this case, sand – that protected patrol bases all over Afghanistan. Tested against charges of up to 20,000lb, the HESCO system was, quite literally, bombproof.

Liam agreed with Clint. The countless HESCOs around the walls gave no indication of what the building inside had once been. That the compound *had* walls was about all the place had going for it, thought Liam, dropping his kit down. It was little better than a tidy building site. Most of the walls were not only reinforced on the outside with sandbags, but on the inside too, as well as with botched struts made from scrap pieces of wood doing their best to stop the place falling in on itself. During its occupation by UK troops, various shelters had been erected, oddly shaped constructions built from scaffolding, scraps of wooden crates, and canvas tarpaulin. Liam had seen pictures, short films, of refugee camps in war zones. This looked worse. And dust and dirt covered everything.

The cookhouse was to his right. A pile of stacked food tins, a trestle table with gas burners, and lots of over-sized aluminium cooking pots. Fresh food was going to be a rare thing once again. Next to this was the jokingly called mess, a collection of old tables and chairs for use during meals or when just grabbing a brew.

In the far right corner was what Liam assumed was called 'the gym'. He'd heard about one soldier employed by the MOD to travel around from compound to compound delivering a gym in a bag. Costing about six hundred quid, each bag contained enough simple fitness kit for any compound, checkpoint or whatever to get set up with a fitness area within minutes. Such an area was vital, not just to help the soldiers keep fit, but also to give them somewhere to let off steam. The kit contained head guards and gloves for just that reason. Sometimes, having a good scrap with a mate was the best therapy any soldier could wish for. It also enabled them to practise unarmed combat. Because, as Liam and the rest knew, no matter how many moves you knew, how many clever ways to block a punch or take someone out, when a real fight happened, it was ninety-five per cent survival, and five per cent getting just such a move right enough to give you the upper hand and get ahead of what your opponent was thinking.

Sadly, though, Liam thought, this place had not yet been reached, and instead everything was home-made, courtesy of squaddie ingenuity. The best example was the weights – a row of scaffold bars, at the end of which were various sizes of tins filled with concrete. There were a number of pull-up bars, some push-up bars too, but that was about it.

'So where do we doss down?' asked Clint.

'Over there, I reckon,' said Liam, nodding left, not an

ounce of enthusiasm in his voice. 'Under that huge grey tarpaulin and past the sitting area.'

As they walked over, Liam spotted Nicky. Being the only woman out there, she got separate quarters and extra privacy.

The multiple that Liam and the others were replacing had cleared their kit out, but Liam didn't trust them. Pulling pranks was part of a soldier's life, and he took some time in sorting out his bed, double-checking it for any lurking surprises.

It was just as Liam was finally sorted, his kit all in good order, that a yell came out from close by.

It was Clint.

11

Liam whipped round. Had Clint been shot at? It was enough to get his heart racing again, as he immediately did a 360 scan, looking for anywhere a sniper could get a shot in, even though he knew they were safe in the compound. If someone had, like Hammond had suggested, leaked intelligence, then anything was possible. As he did so, he caught sight of something huge in the air in front of Clint, something he was trying to slap away from his chest. He stepped back, stumbled into his bed, and fell. Still yelling.

All Liam saw was that Clint was in trouble, and whatever the cause, he was going to sort it out. He jumped over his own bed and dashed across. It was only then, when he was up close, that he realized what the problem was.

'Don't move!' he hissed. 'The fucker might still be alive!'

Clint went deathly still. Liam pulled out his bayonet.

'What the hell are you doing?'

'Seriously, don't move . . .'

'But a bayonet? What do you need that for? If you stab me . . .'

'Stop struggling!' Liam whispered. 'You want it to bite you?'

Clint froze, and Liam leaned in closer to the thing on Clint's webbing. It moved, or at least he thought it did. And with a short sharp jab, he pierced it.

Clint was breathing hard and fast.

'Camel spider,' said Liam, examining the creature stuck to the end of his blade. It was clearly dead, probably had been all along. The size of a dinner plate, its body was not far off that of a small rat, and its legs were long and just plain nasty-looking.

Clint sat up. 'It was in my bed,' he said. 'Actually *in* my bed! I put my kit down and somehow flicked the thing up. Nearly brown-trousered myself. Never seen one up close like that before.'

'For a moment there I thought you'd been slotted,' said Liam. 'Shit, I'm jumpy as fuck now.'

He laughed, but it was as much out of relief as it was humour. The smile on his face helped break the hard shell of horror that was suffocating him after the news about Martin – and the possibility that intelligence about their arrival had been leaked to the Taliban.

'Piss funny,' he said, shaking with the mix of emotion, working at keeping his voice calm. 'Honestly, the funniest thing I've seen in months.'

'To you, maybe,' said Clint, clambering back to his feet. 'I hate spiders. Can't stand the things. Make me freak out.'

'They're not technically spiders,' said Liam.

'See my face?' said Clint. 'Look like I care what it is? All I know is it's got lots of legs and crawls.' He shuddered.

'Same thing happened to me last time I was out,' said Liam, remembering finding a dead camel spider in his own bed. 'Their bites can get infected easily, but they're not killers. Creepy, though, aren't they? Proper horror-movie stuff!'

Clint said, 'I hate horror movies.' Then added, 'At least it made you smile.'

Liam shrugged. 'Humour's the only thing that helps keep you sane out here, right?'

It was then, though, that a darker thought stretched out its thin, sly fingers. Liam saw that Clint had noticed a change, heard his laughter die.

'What's wrong?' Clint asked. 'You're sure it's dead, right? It didn't bite you, did it?'

Liam caught a look from some of the lads who'd been here a while, who were clearly envious of their mates in the multiple that had just left. He gave a thumbs up and smiled. They saluted back, clearly proud their little joke had paid off. Thank God it hadn't been anything else, he thought. He needed to chill out, not jump at everything, as that could be dangerous. He also knew he had to be alert. If there was someone somewhere giving information to the Taliban, then it was in everyone's interest to find out who.

Miller scooted over, jarring Liam from his thoughts. 'Scott?'

'I'm OK, boss,' said Liam, registering the concern in the sergeant's voice.

'We'll deal with Saunders' stuff later,' said Miller, acknowledging Liam's response with a firm nod. 'Until then, I need people up in the sangars and on the wall. It'll be dark soon enough and I don't want them thinking we're slacking up, just because they've taken out a Chinook and we've suffered casualties. We hammered them hard, but there's always a chance some other fuckers will be back to have a go.'

Liam saw a couple of other lads making their way up some ladders to the lookouts that stared out across the land surrounding the compound.

'So I want you two up there,' said Miller, pointing up

at the wall. 'Stirling and Hammond are up in the other. There's binos up there, a Gimpy, LASWs. Get your eyes in and inform me of anything that moves. Now we're out here, my PRR is on twenty-four seven.'

'Yes, boss,' said Liam.

'What about the Chinook?' asked Clint.

'In hand,' said Miller. 'A secure perimeter is in place. There was a brief contact as we pushed back to secure the HLS, but their heart wasn't in it. They bugged out sharpish. It's being checked over for salvageable kit now. Then we'll finish the job and make sure it's of no use to anyone. Now move it!'

Liam, with Clint following, grabbed his SA80 and zipped across the compound to their designated sangar, a barely standing lookout post with a view from the compound walls and out to the beyond. It was good to be busy so soon, he thought, nearing the ladder. Best thing he could do now was focus on the job in hand.

As Liam grabbed the ladder, he heard Ade swear. Turning, he saw Ade's kit all over the floor thanks to a broken bed.

'You do know it's seriously bad luck to break a bed before you sleep in it,' said Clint. 'From now on, you're a marked man, Ade.'

'Fuck off,' said Ade. 'And what I mean by that is fuck

off, just in case you didn't understand. We've had enough seriously bad luck already.'

'Yeah, we've not even started out here and we've already been hammered, lost a helicopter, suffered injuries. And Saunders . . .' said Liam, starting up the ladder.

'Keep moving,' said Clint, not giving Liam time to dwell on Martin's death, 'I don't like staring at your backside.'

The sangar was built from sandbags, thick enough to hopefully see off a hit from an RPG. The roof was corrugated steel overlaid with more bags. They had a good arc of sight, left to right, and Liam was happy to see that anyone approaching within 300 metres would be pretty easy to spot. That wouldn't stop them trying, though, he knew. There was plenty of scrub and brush in the land beyond the compound, and someone determined and patient enough could slowly creep forward. They'd have to have their eyes tuned into any movement, double-check anything that looked dodgy.

He checked over the GPMG. Capable of 750 rounds a minute, and with a range of up to 1800 metres, the L7AT General-Purpose Machine Gun was the infantry workhorse. It was astonishingly reliable, belt-fed, and fired 7.62 rounds. Liam had used one before. It was deadly.

Clint was on the range-finder binos and doing a

quick sweep of the harsh wilderness that lay before them. It was rough ground, rock and dirt and plants so hardy they could probably survive a nuclear attack. The ground rose in front of them gradually, the horizon dropping off at about 400 metres, and beyond that were distant mountains, their heads covered in a grey shroud of cloud. It was a landscape that was hauntingly quiet. The air was dry and what wind there was simply stirred up the stale aroma of soldiers living closely together and all that entailed. It was a smell you got used to, but never missed.

'Nice area,' Clint said. 'Pretty and rural.'

'The bastards will still be out there,' said Liam, staring down the iron sight of the GPMG, checking his arc of fire left to right, pinpointing any areas he thought had the potential to hide anyone wanting to slip close and have a look-see. He didn't say it, but deep down he was itching to get one back for Martin. And he knew he wouldn't be alone in that. All soldiers felt the same. They were warriors, it was what they did. And if one of their own got hit, then it was a natural thing to want to fight back, and harder.

Clint grabbed a bottle of water from a stash in the sangar, handing another to Liam.

'I guess we're going to be up here a while,' he said. 'Ever played I-spy?'

* * *

It was closing in on three hours later when two other soldiers finally relieved them. Down in the compound, life was busy, with the cookhouse running a late supper, a few lads using the gym area, and the rest keeping themselves busy with anything from stripping weapons to writing home. Rob was, unsurprisingly, listening to his iPod. Liam had his, but found he didn't use it as much as he'd expected. After a while the music grew more annoying than the hustle and bustle of the world around him. Power wasn't a problem either, because if there was one piece of kit all squaddies had it was a solar charger.

'All right, lads,' said Clint, as the two replacements came up top. 'Make yourself at home.'

'You're having a laugh, aren't you?' It was Tim Harding. His bright red hair looked even brighter next to his pale skin; he wasn't exactly built for desert survival. 'We're already fucked.'

Liam caught the remark and threw it back. Soldiers griped – it was all part of the job – but he noticed a real edge to Tim's voice, a bitterness. And he didn't like it.

'Not if you do your job properly, we're not,' he said. 'And by that I mean all of us.'

Tim shook his head. 'You were on the Chinook when

we were hit, right? I mean, how fucking unlucky is that?'

Liam noticed Clint staring at him. Luck had nothing to do with it, he thought, and wondered what Tim knew or suspected, if anything.

'It's what happens,' said Liam, working at staying calm, already taking a dislike to Tim. 'You start talking and thinking like we're already screwed, that's when mistakes are made.'

'Who made you an NCO?'

'I'm just saying, that's all,' said Liam, then softened his voice as best he could, thinking that perhaps he wasn't the only one hit hard by Martin's death. 'Just don't let it get to you, right?'

Tim shook his head. 'Those fuckers were waiting,' he said. 'Knew we were coming, had to. Too many of them to just be hanging around by chance.'

Liam kept quiet. He didn't want to add fuel to Tim's fire, make him even more jittery by agreeing with him or suggesting that he was thinking the same thanks to what Rob had said.

Tim muttered under his breath and turned to the binos.

Walking back to the sleeping area, Liam mentioned Tim's attitude to Clint. 'He's more pissed off than he's got a right to be,' he said. 'We're all in this together.

What's the point of being a moany arse? No use, that, is it?'

'We're not alone in thinking something was up,' said Clint. 'Folk are going to be jittery after the firefight.'

Liam said, 'Give us a hand then to sort Saunders' kit?'

'Honoured to,' said Clint.

Waking the next morning, Liam was surprised that the night had gone by without a single round being fired. After the contact of the previous day, he'd half expected the Taliban to come back to really hammer the message home that visitors were not welcome.

Washed, and with breakfast inside him, Liam was already lining up at the door for a foot patrol with Clint, four lads he knew by name only, and a bloke called James Stirling, who was on point. Armed with a black combat shotgun slung at his side, and carrying a combat metal detector, James had the look of an excited puppy about him, his face always bright and keen, but that was partly the fault of his eyes, which were blue and shone with a laser brightness beneath caramel-coloured hair. All that Liam really knew about James was that he liked to dance. He didn't even need music. And he was doing it now, head moving side to side, feet doing a jig, like he'd swallowed an iPod and couldn't turn it off. Nicky was with them too. Liam was glad. He'd seen just how well she worked under fire.

Their role here was different from Liam's first tour. It wasn't just foot patrols, like he was used to. Instead, they would be visiting a number of Afghan patrol bases and checkpoints throughout the Yakchal, and up and down Highway One. The aim was to spend a day or two at each base, work alongside the ANA, then head back to Patrol Base 1 between each visit. And they would be getting to each of the ANA patrol bases by foot and by vehicle.

Miller, having gone through today's route with them half an hour before, marking it all out on the ground as best he could, was leading the show. Lance Corporal Clark was also with them, the Fijian with a hard face and hands like shovels. Liam had yet to hear him say much. All he knew was that the NCO was a crack shot and was carrying the Sharpshooter. He would be bringing up the rear.

With them were four ANA soldiers, one of them a gruff-faced officer who looked hard enough to split granite with a stare. They were from the nearest of the Afghan PBs and were here for additional training and experience, to give the new arrivals some immediate experience of working with the ANA, and to help build and improve working relationships between the British forces and the locals. It was both political and sensible. No one was complaining. Anything that helped get the job done was good in any soldier's eyes.

'This is our first patrol,' said the sergeant, with everyone gathered around. 'You've all seen the route,' he continued. 'This is to show face more than anything. Let all those fuckers who joined in yesterday, and who are probably keeping a watch on us, see that we're here for the duration and don't take any crap. We'll be out for two hours, following the track that leads out beyond the front of the compound and over the ridge. I want us all to have a good idea of the land around us and to identify possible areas the Taliban may use to sneak up and cause trouble.'

Liam liked Miller more and more. He was a straight-talking soldier and obviously knew his job inside and out.

'We're here to help keep this place secure,' said Miller, 'work with the locals, and help the ANA eventually take control when we move out. We'll do foot patrols to start, get our eye in and show that we're here to do our job, not hide away behind these walls. Then we'll be moving out to other Afghan PBs in the Foxhounds. Any questions?'

No one spoke.

'Right, then, let's get a fucking move on, eh? Move out!'

The door to the compound opened. With James out front, the rest following behind, Liam was out in the open and back on patrol.

Liam was acutely aware of how his senses heightened with each step he made. The air, dry and laced with the scent of grass and pollen, carried with it endless squalls of dust, which whipped up around the patrol's feet, chasing them as they went. Far off, mountains rose like huge fossilized teeth. The clouds were high, dotting the blue sky with smudges of white. It was beautiful country, he thought. Harsh, unforgiving, but still beautiful. And it all seemed so at odds with the violence and terror going on within its borders, a violence that wasn't just part of what had happened with the Taliban, but stretched back centuries. Afghanistan was a country unconquered and unconquerable. Liam thought how that would probably never really change, no matter what anyone did.

No one was speaking, and with it being a first patrol, Liam was pleased. It meant everyone was focused on what they were doing. Out here, the risk of attack was clear and present, be it from a sniper, an ambush or an IED. And every step further away from the compound was another step away from relative safety.

One thing that impressed him was the ANA soldiers. He had expected them to be a ragtag bunch, with shoddy kit and a not exactly professional attitude. The opposite was true. They were well-armed with the American M16s and were working the patrol as well as the others. If anything, he thought, probably better. They knew this land and knew what to look for.

'Hold!'

It was James. His hand was up and the patrol obeyed, stopping dead still.

Liam watched as James edged forward, metal detector sweeping with slow, deliberate arcs. A few moments later, he walked back to Miller. Liam couldn't hear any words, but it was clear that James had found something.

Miller signalled down the line and one of the ANA moved forward. He was slight in build, and walked with a relaxed air, almost as though he was out for a Sunday stroll, his feet seeming to glide across the ground rather than take steps. Slung over his shoulder was a canvas bag. He was clean-shaven and, when he stopped to speak to Miller, the ANA officer and Stirling, Liam saw that he was smiling, like he was just happy to be alive and doing his job.

'Right, everyone,' called Miller, 'let's back up, keeping

to the cleared path, no veering off.'

Everyone obeyed, coming to a stop about two hundred metres back the way they'd come.

'What's happening?' Liam asked Clint, as they stood watching.

'IED,' said Clint.

'We'll be out here ages, then,' said Liam. 'Counter IED team will be on their way from Camp Bastion. We'll have to wait it out till the IED's made safe.'

'Then what's he doing?' said Clint, gesturing towards the ANA soldier who'd strolled past. He was now up to where James's combat metal detector had done its job and brought the patrol to a halt.

Liam couldn't make out exactly what the man was doing, but he was crouched down and fiddling with something on the ground. He wasn't wearing the protective kit usually associated with bomb disposal so there was no way he could be messing with a possible IED, though what else he could have been doing, Liam hadn't a clue.

A few minutes later the ANA soldier was on his feet and strolling back to the rest of the patrol. And a couple of seconds after he passed Sergeant Miller, an explosion rammed itself hard into the quiet of the day.

Liam couldn't believe it.

'Did he just do what I think he did?' Clint asked.

Liam nodded. 'The mad bastard!' he said, staring at the dirt and grit raining down around where the IED had detonated. 'He wasn't wearing protection and didn't even lie down to miss the blast if it went off!'

The ANA soldier grinned at Miller and sauntered back down the line, stopping next to Liam. Liam stared at him. 'It is safe now,' said the soldier. 'A simple device. No problem.'

Liam was doubly impressed – the soldier's English was excellent. 'But you weren't wearing the suit,' he said, thinking about the kit that the bomb disposal lads had to work in. 'You could've been blown to pieces!'

'Too big,' said the soldier. 'Better like this. Easier to move, see?' He wiggled a little and grinned.

Was this guy for real? thought Liam. Or did he just have a death wish?

'Then why didn't you lie down?'

Liam knew that when an IED went off, the explosion came out in a V shape. Lying down reduced the risk of being hit by the V of deadly shrapnel as it blasted outwards.

'Better to keep clothes clean,' came the reply. 'Washing is expensive.' He smiled again. And it was genuine.

Liam shook his head, smiled back, had nothing left to say.

Miller called from the front for the patrol to move

on. Stirling was back out in front.

Liam, still trying to comprehend what they'd all just witnessed, made to move off, when something thunked into the ground between him and Clint.

'*Contact!*'

12

The round had come from Liam's left and he dropped to one knee and had his weapon in the shoulder. He scanned the horizon. It reminded him of pictures he'd seen of the moon, except with the addition of a few scraggly plants. They didn't know if it was a lone shooter or simply the first shot fired by a group who were readying themselves for a scrap. He was aware now not just of those with him, but of the sound of every small movement, the creak of a boot, rub of clothing, knock of weapon. Someone was out there, could see them, and they had to find them and return fire before a round hammered home and injured someone, or worse.

'No firing unless contact confirmed!' yelled Lance Corporal Clark from the back of the line. 'Remember your ROE! We don't just go spraying rounds everywhere!'

He wasn't being a ball-breaker, Liam knew, but just

sending out a reminder. And it made sense to do that. This was a first patrol. Everyone wanted it to go by the book, even when things turned to shit and a firefight was on.

The silence made Liam hyper aware of his every breath and movement.

'Anything?' Miller up front, shouting back. They were all out with PRRs, but at this range Liam heard the sergeant's voice in the air as well as through the earpiece he was wearing.

No one replied. The ground and undergrowth were refusing to give anything away.

Liam kept scanning, looking for anywhere that might hide an enemy combatant. A bush, a broken dead tree, some rocks. Trouble was, everything was so far out, the landscape so similar wherever you looked, that spotting anything that looked out of place was next to impossible, and the give-away straight line of a barrel easily disguised.

A bright red and yellow flash, 150 metres, max.

'RPG!'

Christ, thought Liam, dropping to the ground, *do the Taliban use anything else?* But at least it had given away the position.

By luck, or simply through poor handling of the weapon, the RPG drifted right and detonated some way off, taking out a tree. Wood blasted up into the air, and the tree wobbled for a moment, then slumped down to the ground like it was drunk. Not that it mattered what damage the rocket had done. The flash had given away the enemy's position. They'd all seen it.

'Have it!'

Miller's call to arms was almost unnecessary as every soldier opened fire, drilling the place with round after round after round.

'Stop!'

The patrol fell silent. Everyone remained vigilant, scanning every blade of grass for a sign of attack. Then Miller directed an advance on the position. It was slow work as James was on point again, checking every step, protected by sustained covering fire from everyone else on where the RPG had been fired from, and the surrounding ground.

James stopped, hoisted his shotgun into his hands, pumped a round into the chamber. He edged forward, then, after a pause, he turned and signalled to Miller.

The contact was over.

Liam checked his watch. It wasn't even lunch time. It was going to be a long, hot and tiring first day out on patrol.

* * *

After the initial violence of their arrival and first day, the rest of the week passed with relative ease. Everyone was greatly relieved. It allowed them to get used to their surroundings, and to deal with the comedown of no longer having access to the facilities that had been afforded them back at Camp Bastion.

The compound was a busy place, and Liam did his best to make himself feel at home as much as possible. He arranged his sleeping area so that it had enough of his stuff on display to show that it was his. It was the little touches that mattered, which was a good thing, really, he thought, because he didn't actually have much. There were still echoes of that first day, though, and he knew he wasn't the only one on edge because of it. Such a firefight didn't just have its effect in the rounds flying; it seeped on through future days, always there in people's minds.

The Taliban had been waiting.

Not that anyone said it outright, because everyone knew the only thing a rumour was good for was distracting people from what they were supposed to be doing.

Checking out some of the other beds, Liam saw family photos, pictures drawn by children, postcards. Clint's were on show again and Liam could see the look of their father in the eyes of both children; a mischievous glint coupled with boundless energy. Liam's only family were his parents. And he didn't really get on with them. Well, not his dad at any rate, and his mum was almost a ghost. They'd turned up to see him get his medal, but that was the last time he'd seen them. And contact with them had been minimal. So, in the end, all he had on display was a few photos from his training and first tour. They were good memories, not least because Cameron was in most of them.

Liam was rearranging the photographs when he sensed someone was watching him. He looked over his shoulder to find that it was the ANA who'd dealt with the IED. Again, Liam was struck by the openness of the soldier's expression. He wasn't guarded at all. It was a little unnerving. Why would anyone be like that? Liam thought. Every soldier he'd met, no matter how open or friendly at first, always kept something back until they really got to know each other. Not that it took long – having people trying to kill you made you become friends pretty quickly. This ANA, though, didn't seem to have anything to hide and Liam found it was almost too easy to relax in his presence. It was uncanny.

'*Salaam*,' said the soldier.

Liam noticed immediately the different greeting. If it was Pashto, he would have expected *salaamu alaikum*, not simply *salaam*. He didn't want to appear ignorant, and managed to pull from his mind the little Dari he'd managed to learn alongside the Pashto.

'*Salaam*,' he replied, and added, '*Chetoor astayn?*'

'*Khoob astum*,' came the reply: 'I am very well indeed!' The soldier grinned, and Liam was pleased his pronunciation of the Dari for *How are you?* had been sufficiently clear. 'You speak Dari!'

Liam laughed and shook his head, then pulled out the phrase book from a pocket. 'Still learning,' he said.

The soldier nodded at the photo. 'He is a close friend?'

'Yes, he was,' said Liam.

'Ah, I understand,' came the reply. 'I am truly sorry.'

Liam stood quietly for a moment, unsure what to say next. The loss of Cam was still with him. And Martin's death had not only caused its own shockwave, but also opened that wound afresh, not that it had yet been given a decent chance to heal. He wasn't sure he wanted it to, because the scars of a friendship like that were something to be proud of. And he didn't want to be suspicious, but really he didn't know this ANA at all; none of them did. They'd all seen him do his job, and well, but that was it.

'He was a good mate,' said Liam, words not coming easy, not really sure what or how much to say.

The soldier walked over to Liam. 'I am Zaman Shah.'

'Scott,' said Liam.

Zaman smiled warmly. 'It is always hard losing someone,' he said. 'Whatever you believe, that is always the same. It is never easy.'

'I guess,' said Liam. 'I've always thought once you're dead that's it, you're gone. But it's hard to believe sometimes. Cam was too alive to be just gone. Still doesn't seem real.'

'This war has taken many lives,' said Zaman. 'Each death is a sadness. Again, I am truly sorry.'

'Thank you,' said Liam, and there was that openness, he thought, drawing him in, making him relax without even realizing it. This Zaman should be an interrogator, he thought – he could get anyone to talk just by looking at them.

'I too have lost many friends,' said Zaman, and for the first time Liam saw a shadow pass over his eyes. There was a darkness behind the friendly smile. Zaman had lived this war, thought Liam, not just survived it. 'Many of my family. I sometimes think our country will never know real peace.'

'I hope it does,' said Liam. 'It's a beautiful place, despite all this.'

Zaman grinned broadly, the darkness Liam had noticed burned away in a second by that smile. 'Thank you!' he said, then asked, 'Have you had kehwa?'

'Er, no,' said Liam, having no idea what Zaman was talking about.

'Come!' Zaman replied. 'Join me!'

Liam checked the time and was amazed to find that his fifth day was already drawing to a close. With nothing else pressing, and realizing that getting to know Zaman was probably a good idea anyway, Liam followed him across the compound to where the ANA lads had settled down.

Zaman asked Liam to sit down then walked over to where Liam had seen the ANA soldiers preparing their food and drink. Whatever it was, it definitely smelled better than what he'd been eating lately. The food at Camp Bastion didn't count – that was restaurant stuff with fresh supplies. Out here, not so much.

Zaman came over to Liam carrying a small and very ornate glass cup, sitting on an equally fragile-looking saucer. 'This is kehwa,' he said, presenting the cup to Liam with an almost reverential air. 'It is green tea. We prepare it with saffron, cinnamon and cardamom and sweeten it with honey.'

'It smells amazing,' said Liam, taking the glass from Zaman. 'Oh, it's hot!'

Zaman nodded. '*Lutfan*,' he said, and Liam was happy to recognize the Dari for *please*. 'It is good, trust me!'

Liam wasn't used to hot drinks in the Afghan heat. And the only drink he really fantasized about was an ice-cold beer, despite the headaches he'd suffered during his recent so-called holiday.

'*Tashakur*,' he said. 'Thank you.' And took a sip. It was hot, but not scalding. 'That's actually delicious.'

'Yes,' said Zaman. 'You must share this with me and my friends.' He called over to two other ANA soldiers. 'This is Scott,' he said, as they arrived and sat down. 'He finds our country beautiful!'

The ANA soldiers beamed at Liam like he'd given them the greatest compliment possible.

'And the kehwa?' asked one, looking to Zaman then Liam.

'It's great,' said Liam, and tried some more. 'Really nice. Proper delicious.'

Taking another sip, he noticed Tim heading back up to the wall. He was staring across at him, his expression grave, disapproving almost. Whatever his problem was, Liam thought, he wasn't going to let it bother him, so he raised his glass to him, then finished it.

Zaman's smile grew even broader, and before Liam could argue a tray of kehwa was brought over and soon they were all drinking and smiling.

The following day, early afternoon, Liam had found

himself relaxing a little after the initial arrival and firefight. Martin's loss was still raw, but he wasn't as edgy, at least not about the thought that someone had leaked intelligence about their arrival. It had been quiet since then and he was fairly confident that whether their arrival had been leaked or not, they'd hit back so hard during the contact that the Taliban had decided to steer clear.

He was over in the gym area when a visitor arrived, bringing with him additional supplies for the compound. Following a stocktake ordered by Lieutenant Steers it had been discovered that more than a few necessary items were running low, including water and medical supplies. A call to Camp Bastion, which everyone had heard – thanks to the lieutenant making his needs starkly clear to whoever had drawn the short straw and answered – and fresh supplies had been quickly arranged.

Sitting up in his bed, Liam stared across the compound at the new arrival. He clocked the dog collar immediately.

'Fuck me, a sky pilot,' said Ade.

'What?'

'A padre. Head in the clouds, talking to his boss,' said Ade. 'If you believe in any of that bollocks.'

'You don't, then?'

'Dead's dead,' said Ade. 'This is all there is. Can't be doing with wasting my time talking to an imaginary friend.'

Lieutenant Steers met the padre with a firm handshake.

'Why's he here?' Liam asked.

'They do the rounds,' said Ade. 'Improve our morale, give us a shoulder to cry on, I guess.'

'Don't knock it,' said Liam.

'Actually, I'm not,' said Ade, for the first time sounding to Liam like he wasn't about rip into something. 'I've seen those blokes with lads who are injured. They don't just sit in safety, they'll do their job under fire. Don't even carry weapons. I might not believe like they do, but I respect them.'

Liam was speechless.

Clint, who'd had his head in a book, said, 'And you need a good cry, do you, Ade? Is that it?'

'Fuck off, Cowboy,' said Ade.

And Ade was back to being himself, Liam thought with a smile. The lieutenant was now walking towards them. Liam swung off his bunk and stood up.

'This is Major Peter Clements,' said the lieutenant, standing in front of them. 'Army padre. He'll be with us for a couple of days. So make him feel at home, yes?'

'Sir,' said Liam.

The major wasn't how Liam would ever have expected a man of the church to look or act. If he'd been told a padre was on his way, he'd have expected someone grey, old and weak to turn up – a person who meant well but would have been better staying at home eating crumpets and talking to old ladies. Major Clements was anything but.

'Hello,' he said, stretching out a hand for Liam to shake. 'I know we're supposed to stick to all that military convention stuff, but I'd prefer it if you just called me Pete.'

Liam took the padre's hand and almost wished he hadn't; the grip was strong. 'I'm Scott,' he said. 'The bald one's Eastwood, and that's Sunter.'

'So how are you settling in?'

'It's fucking brilliant,' said Ade. 'Luxury! Though I wouldn't mind some softer bog roll; my arse is red raw.'

'I'm fresh out,' said Pete. 'I'm sorry.'

'Didn't God tell you?'

'Did you ask him?' replied Pete, raising an eyebrow.

Ade laughed. It was a rare thing to hear, thought Liam.

'So where can someone grab a brew?' the padre asked. 'I'm gasping.'

'I'll take you,' said Liam, pointing over to where they

all sat down for their much-needed, if not always that palatable, scoff. 'The mess is over there.'

'The mess?' said Pete when they arrived at what was simply a collection of mis-matched chairs dotted around some pallets, now given a new life as impromptu tables.

Liam laughed. 'Well, that's what we call it,' he said. Grabbing a couple of mugs of tea, he sat down with the padre.

'I hear it was a tough start,' Pete said, taking a sip. 'Good tea, by the way. First decent one I've had in days.'

Liam said nothing, just took a sip himself.

'Don't worry,' said Pete, and Liam could tell that he'd picked up on his own silence. 'I'm not here to pry. But if you need to talk about what happened, or anything really, I'm a good listener.'

Liam wasn't sure how to respond. 'Thanks,' he said at last, then asked, 'So were you always a padre?'

Pete laughed. 'Not a chance,' he said.

'Oh, right,' said Liam. 'I just assumed . . .'

Pete rolled up his right sleeve and Liam saw a tattoo. It was the cap badge of the Parachute Regiment.

'Holy fuck . . .'

Pete laughed out loud. 'That's one way of putting it.'

'You were a Para?'

Pete nodded. 'I was in Iraq first time round,' he

said. 'Fresh out of training too. Quite the learning curve.'

Liam was impressed. Becoming a Para was no easy task. One of his mates back at Harrogate had joined and he'd been the fittest bloke Liam had ever met. And tough.

'How long were you in for?'

'Long enough,' said Pete. 'When I finally decided to leave the army, I discovered God had other plans.'

Liam finished his tea. 'Martin was a good lad,' he said.

'So I hear,' said Pete.

Liam smiled, remembering their flight into Camp Bastion. 'Everyone called him Mascot because he was so small. He was keen too. Wouldn't stop asking questions. It was shit, the way he got killed, you know?'

'Yes, I do know,' said Pete, and Liam could tell that he meant it. 'The death of a friend – it's something you never really get over.'

Liam nodded. 'Lost a mate last time I was out here,' he said. 'And back home.'

'Back home?' asked Pete. 'That's tough.'

'It's the reason I'm here, I guess,' said Liam.

'You were close?'

'Yes,' said Liam. 'Knew each other since we were kids.'

'What happened?'

Liam found himself liking the padre more and more. In a way, he reminded him of Zaman – the way he somehow put him at ease, made him want to talk.

'It was an accident,' Liam explained, remembering seeing his friend Dan fall while they'd been out messing around with some free running in a derelict factory. 'I was with him when he died. Kind of puts things into perspective.'

'Death does that,' said Pete. 'Look, I'm going to do a memorial this evening. If there's anything you can tell me about Martin, I'd love to hear it. I always prefer these things to be personal. Martin was a person, you all knew him. He deserves it to be real, if you know what I mean.'

A shout came from the gym area. It was Lance Corporal Clark.

'What's going on?' Pete asked, glancing over.

'Clark's decided to run regular fitness competitions,' said Liam, finishing his mug of tea.

'You entering?'

'No, but Sunter is,' said Liam. 'Seems to think he'll win easily. But that's only because Clint's not in on it, otherwise he wouldn't have a chance. Coming?'

'Of course,' said Pete and stood up. 'After you?'

Over at the gym, Ade clocked the major. 'Soldiers only,' he said. 'Don't want you to get hurt now, do we, Padre? Might damage those wings of yours.'

Liam started to speak but the major stepped in and said, 'It wouldn't be fair anyway.'

'Too right,' said Ade. 'Men of steel we are, hey, lads?' A ripple of laughter went round the soldiers.

'No, I meant on you,' said Pete.

'You're funny for a padre,' said Ade.

Clark said, 'Join in if you want, Padre. Entirely up to you. The winner gets the admiration of his peers and the chance to set the next competition.'

To cheers, the major stepped forward. 'So, what's the test?'

'Press-ups,' Cowell answered. 'Max. Just keep going till you drop.'

'Sounds simple.'

'Like Sunter,' said Clint, standing next to Liam.

Ade snarled. 'Come on then, Padre, you can go next to me.'

'This I have to see,' said Clint.

'Me too,' agreed Liam.

'You know something I don't?' asked Clint.

Liam smiled, said nothing.

A minute or so later, Major Pete Clements was one of six soldiers down and ready in a press-up position. Six others were on the floor beside them, fists under each soldier's chest to count the reps.

'You can give up now if you want,' said Ade, looking at the major. 'No shame in it – know what I mean?'

'Thank you,' he replied. 'But I'm here now, so I may as well see if I can do a few at least.'

Lance Corporal Clark called everyone to order. 'Rules are simple. Do as many full press-ups as you can. Just keep going till you drop. Ready?'

A chorus of: 'Yes, Corporal!'

'Then on my mark . . . *GO!*'

As one, the soldiers raced into the press-ups. Liam knew none of them wanted to be the first to drop out, and when the first did, he regretted it immediately as his failure was met with howls of laughter.

'Sunter's fitter than I thought,' said Clint.

'Fit, or just worried he's going to get his arse kicked by a padre?' said Liam.

Another of the soldiers dropped, and the next two followed quickly, leaving just Ade and, to everyone's astonishment, Major Clements.

'I thought you were good,' said Liam to Clint. 'But the padre doesn't even seem out of breath.'

With only two left, everyone started to cheer them on. Liam could see Ade was pushing hard now. He was huffing and puffing, his face red, the veins on his arms like wire cables under his skin.

Then it happened: his arms froze and he just couldn't move.

'Come on! Don't give up! Move it!' Clint yelled, but it was no good. Just a few seconds later, Ade dropped onto his chest.

The padre, however, kept going.

Ade sat up. 'What did I manage?' He was out of breath, sucking air into his lungs, the pain of exertion etched onto his face, his arms shaking as his muscles tried to recover.

'One hundred and thirty-two,' said Clark. 'That's seriously good. Well done. Didn't think you had it in you, to be fair. You always look like a weedy bastard.'

Ade looked at the padre, as did Liam. He still hadn't stopped. His pace was steady, unstoppable almost, like he could just go on for ever. A few seconds later, Ade asked, 'And what's he on now?'

'Hundred and seventy-four.'

'Holy shit . . .'

'Literally,' said Clint.

At last Major Clements stopped. He was sweating hard, but still didn't look as broken as Ade had when he'd finally dropped onto his face. 'I think that's two hundred, yes?' he said calmly.

Clark looked at the soldier who had been counting for the padre. He got a nod. 'It would seem so,' he said.

Pete stood up, then reached a hand down to Ade, helping him to his feet. 'Thanks for that,' he said. 'Better luck next time?'

Ade was a picture of disbelief. 'You're a fit son of a bitch.'

The major winked. 'Now, how about another cup of tea for the victor?'

13

'Thank you,' said Liam, walking over to the padre. 'What you said last night, it was great. Saunders would've liked it. I'm sure of it.'

It was the day after the padre had arrived and, as promised, he had carried out a service in memory of Martin Saunders. Liam knew that by now Martin's body would have been repatriated to the UK in the back of a C17. But the memory of him was still there. Liam hadn't been the only one who'd cried either. And no one had thought to rib him for doing so. This was the death of a comrade, and that kind of thing affected everyone deep down. It brought the reality of their job home, and did it harder than anything. Tears, if anything, thought Liam, were a proper sign of respect to the person gone. They showed exactly how much everyone had thought of Martin.

The major smiled. 'Thank you, Scott,' he said.

'Memorial services are difficult. I'm always nervous of saying the wrong thing or not getting the details right.'

'It was spot on,' said Liam, and could feel himself getting choked up again. But he managed to hold the tears back. He'd let them flow the night before and that had been fair enough. Now, though, it was back to the job and staying alive.

'I have you in part to thank for that,' replied the major and handed Liam back a piece of paper. 'You write well, you know? And loss is generally something most people struggle to express in words.'

Liam took the paper, which was covered with some handwritten notes he'd put together about Martin at the padre's request, and pushed it into a pocket. He didn't want to talk about it any more. Thinking about Martin, writing it down, had brought back dark memories of Cameron's death. Funny, though; just being able to mention Cam again, to the padre, had made him feel better, made him feel he was beginning to come to terms with it. Like he might not kick off so easily at a wanker in a bar again.

'When do you leave?'

'This afternoon, I think,' replied the padre. 'Certainly more interesting than running a little village parish back home.' He laughed. 'Imagine if I landed on the vicarage lawn in a Chinook?'

* * *

That evening, with the padre on his way to another group of soldiers somewhere in the Afghan desert, Liam was sitting in the mess with Clint. Ade was there too, re-reading an old climbing magazine, playing with a karabiner.

'He's still smarting from the bucketload of whoop-ass he got handed by the padre,' said Clint, nodding over at Ade.

Liam laughed, then spotted Lieutenant Steers approaching.

'Scott,' said the lieutenant, sitting down.

'Sir.'

'I spoke to the padre earlier. Told me that you'd helped him with what he said at Saunders' memorial. Can't have been easy. Well done.'

'Thank you,' said Liam.

'Well,' said the lieutenant, 'keep it up.' He stood, then glanced at Ade, who had now plugged his ears with earphones. 'Should I tell him the padre's little secret or not?'

Liam and Clint looked at each other. 'Secret?' said Liam. 'What? That he was in the Paras?'

'That's some secret,' said Clint. 'Explains a lot. Top effort!'

'That's true,' said the lieutenant.

'Not your average padre, then,' said Clint.

'No, not really,' said the lieutenant. 'It was after the Paras that he had his calling, as it were.'

'He left the army and came back?' said Clint.

The lieutenant shook his head. 'Not exactly. From the Paras he went on and passed Selection. John Clements, Padre, is also ex-SAS.'

For the next few days, the routine was the same: manning the sangars, using the gym, eating at the cookhouse, and getting their heads down. There were regular patrols, with a good majority of them involving interaction with locals to improve relations between them and the security forces in the area. Liam got to know Zaman better as the days went on, and made good use of their conversations to practise his Dari. His pronunciation often made Zaman laugh, but it was always well meaning, and Liam quickly found that he was understanding more and able to join in with at least a few broken phrases. Then at last came the time to head out in the two Foxhounds to the first ANA patrol base.

Liam had seen Foxhounds around Camp Bastion, but hadn't thought that he'd be getting to use one. The Foxhound, designed and built in Britain, had been field-tested in Helmand before being deployed. It was, thought Liam, fully rock-and-roll awesome. It looked mean, had a top speed of 70mph and provided outstanding levels of blast protection, thanks to its V-shaped hull. It could even drive away from an attack on only three wheels.

The trip out of the old police station and to their next home was like a white-knuckle ride at a pleasure park. Liam wasn't sure of the distance – it was probably only twenty kilometres – but it took for ever to get there, the vehicles driving at a careful speed, the drivers focusing on the road ahead, always aware that an IED could be anywhere. No amount of checking could ever guarantee a road was completely clear. But there was no point dwelling on the potential hazards or you'd go mad and never leave the compound.

In the back of the first truck, Liam and the others were strapped in, but that didn't stop them being bumped around like crazy. They arrived bruised but safe, with no problems along the way at all, thanks to the route being recce'd the night before. That in itself was reassuring. Liam knew just how capable the Foxhound was, but that didn't mean he necessarily wanted those capabilities to be tested out – to see if it really *could* pull away on three wheels.

Climbing out of the vehicle, his body achingly numb after all the bumps and knocks along the way, he rested his eyes on their new accommodation. The ANA patrol base was small, and seemed even more so sitting completely alone in a huge flat desert plain. The land immediately surrounding it had been cleared of all vegetation, giving anyone inside clear line of sight for about two hundred metres. Where the open ground stopped, the shrubs were rough and hardy and dry. Again, Liam was struck by the harshness of the place and wondered how anyone could live here, never mind a whole society grow and thrive over hundreds of years.

As they walked towards the patrol base, everything was covered in dust, the ground all grit and stone. The outside of the compound showed the telltale signs of attack from small arms and RPGs, with chunks knocked out of it, yet still it stood resolutely against further attack. If anything, it looked bullheadish and stubborn, almost as though it was staring out and daring someone to come and have another go. Worryingly, though, realized Liam, the place lacked the serious protection of HESCOs, depending more on piles of sandbags. They did the job, but often only just.

Quickly settling in, their sleeping area completely separate to the ANA stationed there, Liam was pleased to at least be on the move. This may have been little different to the previous patrol base, but that didn't really matter. Keeping busy coupled with a change of scene was good, kept people fresh and alert.

Lieutenant Steers worked well with Miller, Cowell and Clark, and the ANA, to ensure everyone was kept occupied. And that didn't just involve reviewing their operating procedures, how the patrol base was run, and the patrols. Everyone was given tasks to keep the compound in good order, and no one complained because they were all in the same boat. Rotas were put in place to run the cookhouse, tidy up, report back to Camp Bastion, organize entertainment, such as fitness competitions, and to sort out the disposable latrines. These were bags filled with a gel, similar to that used in nappies, that could then be burned. There was no sewage system here and running water didn't exist.

Most days brought with them some form of contact, from random pot shots and IEDs, to full-on night attacks. Amazingly, despite this, the only casualties yet were the ones from that first day at the HLS. Liam wondered how long such luck would last.

He was cleaning his SA80 and getting his kit together when Lieutenant Steers called him over. Liam had noticed that the lieutenant kept a close eye on everyone in his charge. Not in a bad, suffocating way, but with a firm, professional eye on due care and attention. It was obvious that he lived and breathed his job. And that was exactly how any soldier wanted an officer to be.

'So, how are you, Scott?'

'OK,' said Liam, then added, 'It's good to be back, sir. I'm glad I transferred.'

'So am I,' replied Steers. 'I've been impressed with your focus, particularly considering the loss we all experienced when we arrived out of Camp Bastion.'

Liam said nothing, just nodded.

'You knew Saunders only a short time, but he clearly looked up to you. So thank you for sorting out his kit back there. It was appreciated.'

'No problem,' said Liam, then added, 'Sir.'

It was clear to Liam that the lieutenant was putting him at ease. And he was doing this for a specific reason, but what?

'I'll come straight to the point,' said the lieutenant. 'As you know, we are here to work with the ANA, to help them with their patrols, deal with the Taliban and so on. From here on in our life gets more interesting.'

'Sir,' said Liam, wondering where this was going.

'Well, today Harper is visiting a local village. We're going along with an ANA patrol. Relations between the ANA and the locals are good there.'

Liam said nothing, just listened.

'Also, I've noticed you've struck up a good working relationship with Shah.'

'Yes,' said Liam. 'He's helped me with my Dari. Not that I've had to use it much, but it's fun learning.'

'Agreed,' said the lieutenant. 'I've overheard you talking. Seems to me that you have an aptitude for languages.'

Liam was taken aback. 'I'm not so sure about that, sir.' As far as he was concerned, all he'd done was mix in. They were all living together, so it made sense to get to know Zaman and the others and to learn their language. He'd made use of the MOD-issue phrase book and done his best to strike up conversation, or at least join in with a mix of bad pronunciation and sign language. To have this noticed by anyone was a bit of a shock, and again made him realize just what a good officer Steers was.

'Well, I am, and so is Sergeant Miller,' said the lieutenant. 'And we'd like you to work on it further. As I'm sure you've noticed, the ANA we are working with don't speak Pashto, as they're from this area where Dari is mainly spoken. That you've picked it up so well could come in very useful.'

Liam had actually noticed this already and had got the ANA lads, Zaman particularly, to help him with a few specific phrases. And he was enjoying learning with them. They were a good bunch, and a laugh too.

'It's always helpful to have soldiers who can communicate well with the locals,' said the lieutenant. 'And you might even turn out to be a bit of an ace card for us, for all I know. Will do you good too, I shouldn't say. Excellent stuff for that CV if you want to further your army career after this tour. What do you think?'

'What do I think about what, sir?'

'I'm sending you out on a patrol with Harper,' the lieutenant explained. 'Eastwood, Miller and Harding will be there too. Their role is to run the patrol as normal, observe, collect any intelligence. You, however, will be there specifically to support her, to work with Shah and the locals. I would advise you to do what she asks. As we all know, she's a bit of a ballbreaker, is Harper. Not that any of us would have her any other way.'

Liam smiled. The lieutenant really did seem to know everyone very well indeed.

'As I've said, Zaman Shah will be going with you,' said Steers. 'You clearly get on well, it seems, and we think we may keep him close for that reason, not just here, but when we move to the next PB. Any stability we can give ourselves in being able to deal with whatever we find is always useful. And your help with this, and your clear ability with speaking Dari, will be much appreciated.'

Liam was pleased. He and Zaman were already becoming good friends, the Afghan having a great sense of humour and being not only easy to talk to but very happy to help Liam learn new words and phrases and to practise them with him.

'Should be a nice little jolly, Scott, don't you think?'

'Really, sir? A jolly?'

'The route there is clear,' replied Steers, ignoring Liam's sarcasm, 'and the village very friendly. They kicked the Taliban out months ago and have managed to stay that way, which is no easy task here in Yakchal. You'll be helping Harper give out much-needed medical aid, and at the same time improving your own language skills, and showing the security forces in a positive light.'

'Yes, sir.'

'Good!' said the lieutenant. 'I'm glad you agree. One other thing to be aware of is that weapons may be hidden in or around the village. Nothing to write home about, but be aware of it, just in case.'

'But you just said it was free of the Taliban . . .'

'It is,' said the lieutenant. 'But that is relatively recent in the grand scheme of things. The Taliban may leave, but it's not so clean-cut that once they're gone, that's it. Some may have connections with the village. Family. It's pretty easy to hide an AK47, and even easier to keep its whereabouts secret. See you in half an hour in the mess.'

The village was a battle-scarred collection of typical Afghan dwellings, clustered along a dirt track, which itself was a dot-to-dot of weather-worn craters from IEDs and the scars of long-ago floods. The only colour in the place was from the drapes hung over doors and windows, and Liam could just about make out reds and blues and greens, all stitched into patterns, hiding behind years of dirt and dust. He had no idea when the region had last seen rain, but he knew that when it hit, it came in hard. Often, with the ground so dry, the water would just spill across the surface, building to a flood frighteningly quickly. The houses in the village, if they could be called that, were one-storey buildings mostly built from mud brick, with some parts constructed with oddments of metal and wood. They seemed to rest on the ground like scabs on skin, wounds dried and cracked. Doors and windows were little more than holes covered with planked doors or folds of dusty, worn cloth. Carts that would've looked old in medieval times were dotted here and there.

Entering the village, Liam, like the rest of the patrol, worked hard to look calm and relaxed, while at the same time keeping his eyes and ears tuned in to any sign of a possible threat. The lieutenant may have said the village was friendly and safe, but Liam knew that to let down his guard wasn't just foolish: it was dangerous – to him, and to those he was with. Not only because of what the lieutenant had said about possible hidden weapons, but also because of what Rob had suggested. Liam had found it difficult to shift the thought that someone on their side might be leaking information to the Taliban.

As they walked along, the villagers came out to meet them. Liam nodded, smiled, waved. He saw Clint and Miller do the same. Tim, though, he noticed, didn't seem so relaxed, didn't wave once, his face stern, eyes darting about nervously. Liam wondered how someone like Tim had made it through training, never mind out into theatre. There was something bothering him, that was clear. Not enough to make him a danger to the rest of them, but sufficient to make Liam notice it.

'We're heading up there,' said Nicky, signalling to a building ahead on the left. 'It was a derelict house so they use it as a makeshift medical centre. And trust me – the key word there isn't medical.'

With Nicky leading the way, the rest followed. As they entered the building, Clint, Miller and Tim stayed outside, while Liam, as Lieutenant Steers had ordered, kept alongside Nicky.

'See?' she said, when they walked in. 'Honestly, how these people survive is sometimes beyond me. They're tough, that's for sure.'

The house was derelict, Liam quickly discovered, because half of it had fallen down. The repairs, a mix of bodged rebuilding with oddly balanced wooden beams jostling for position with sheets of corrugated iron, did their job, but barely. Liam couldn't work out how any of it was still standing. However, it had been tidied as best it could be, and a large carpet spread on the floor.

Zaman came over. 'The villagers will make their way over here soon now that they have seen us arrive. I will go and speak to them.' He and the other ANA soldiers then walked across the road to meet an older man halfway. They exchanged greetings and walked into another building.

'That'll be them for a while,' said Nicky and mimed having a drink. 'Tea is a big part of getting to know the locals,' she explained, 'and the ANA lads really help in making sure people are at ease with our presence. They've worked very hard and in very dangerous conditions to get the locals onside. They'll be playing board games in there in a few minutes, I promise you.'

Liam asked Nicky, 'So what exactly are we doing here?'

'Building bridges,' she said, unpacking medical supplies and arranging them on a single rickety table standing in front of them. 'If all they see is soldiers with guns, that is all they will remember – that the violence of the Taliban was replaced by the violence of us.' She held up a plaster. It had a picture of Scooby Doo on it. 'Put this on a young kid's cut knee and you've done more to help the peace process than the US and UK forces put together.'

Liam wasn't so sure that was entirely accurate, but he understood what Nicky was getting at.

A shadow slipped across the floor from the open door and Liam looked up to see a woman bringing in two young boys. Zaman was with her. He entered first, then smiled and beckoned them over, talking gently to them.

'*Salaam aalaikum*,' Liam tried, and the woman lowered her eyes and replied, '*Wa'alaikum salaam*.' Liam was delighted – his first attempt to speak Dari to a non-military Afghan and he had been understood!

'The older boy has a stomach-ache,' said Zaman. 'The younger boy an infected cut on his arm.'

Liam watched as Nicky dealt with the two boys, Zaman helping by constantly reassuring the mother.

'They remind me of my own brother and me,' said Zaman when the family eventually left, both boys sporting Scooby Doo plasters, even though the oldest didn't actually need one.

'My parents only had me,' said Liam. 'If you met them, you'd think it was the best decision they ever made.'

An older man came in, limping badly and leaning on a stick in his right hand. Liam noticed how the man still walked with pride, though, and he wondered how hard it must be for someone like him to ask them for help. A younger man was with him and his eyes were dark, flicking from one soldier to the next nervously. It was obvious to Liam that not only did he hold the older man in great esteem, but also that he didn't trust any of the soldiers, ANA or otherwise.

As the old man drew closer Liam noticed a strong smell, acrid and rotting.

'This is going to be interesting,' said Nicky, as she helped the man to sit down, then started to unravel a dirty bandage on his left leg.

When the bandage finally came off, Liam saw where the smell had come from. The old man had a hole in his calf muscle about the size of a cricket ball. The wound was weeping, bloody and filled with pus. As Liam stared at it, doing his best not to gag, he noticed then that something was moving in it: maggots.

Nicky got on with cleaning it up. 'The maggots are probably what's saved the limb,' she said, gently cleaning the old man's leg. 'They live on the rotten flesh and that will have stopped this getting worse than it is, or slowed it down at any rate.'

The young man hovered around the elder, nervous and jumpy. And whereas the older man smiled gratefully, despite the pain he was clearly suffering, the younger man scowled at everyone in the room with a stare that wanted to burn through them. Liam kept his eyes on him, trusting him about as far as he could spit him. He hadn't said a word, hadn't even offered a greeting, and it was getting more obvious by the second that what he'd read as distrust was more like barely disguised hatred.

'So why did you choose bomb disposal?' Liam asked Zaman, as Nicky wrapped a fresh bandage around the old man's leg.

'It is a useful skill,' said Zaman. 'It saves lives. That is important. Anyone can kill another. I prefer not to.'

'What about your brother?' asked Liam. 'What does he do?'

'He is with the Taliban,' was Zaman's reply.

Liam did a double take, could think of nothing to say.

'Shah?' said Nicky. 'Can you tell them that they need to clean the leg twice a day, and wrap it in a clean bandage.'

Nicky handed the younger man some bandages, who snatched them off her, his lip curled. Zaman did as she requested, explaining what they were for. Then the old man, aided by the younger, made his slow way back out into the street. Again, he was grateful, and again his helper said nothing.

'It is more common than you probably know,' said Zaman, glancing back at Liam.

'What is?' replied Liam, then understood and asked, 'Why didn't he join the ANA with you?'

'It is often down to the wish of the parents what their children do,' said Zaman. 'And it is sensible to think of family.'

'I don't understand.'

'If the Taliban or the ANA win, it does not matter,' said Zaman. 'Whatever happens, whoever wins, the family will survive. That is what is important. Above all else.'

14

It had been unusually quiet for the past few days and Liam was up in a sangar, hands resting on the GPMG. It was mid morning and he was fantasizing about what a proper breakfast would be like. There was often no rhyme or reason as to what they ate, or when, and he was never really surprised to find himself eating pasta at seven in the morning. All he wanted, right then, was a plate piled high with everything a full English was about: eggs and bacon and mushrooms, black pudding and sausages, fried bread and beans. With the daydream making his mouth water, he stared out over the landscape before him.

He had never really been prepared to find the terrain so breath-taking, but it was. He was restless, though. It wasn't that he was desperately looking for the Taliban to come along and have a go, more that he was getting a little edgy. Actually wishing for a fight was something no soldier did. But sometimes the boredom and routine would get to you and you'd yearn for some action.

By now the routine of military life was running like clockwork. Liam knew what to do and when to do it. He kept his kit in good order, had carried out his stints in the cookhouse, and had taken to hanging out more and more with Zaman and the other lads from the ANA because it was not only helping him to improve his Dari and Pashto, but giving him a better understanding of what life was like for the people who lived in this war-ravaged country.

Standing with Liam in the small lookout was Neil Carter. Every movement seemed deliberately posed, like he knew the world was watching and in awe.

'So, GQ, how is it that you always manage to look so clean?' Liam asked, leaning forward against the protective sandbags.

'It's called having a wash,' said Neil, his eyes hidden by a pair of seriously expensive sunglasses, his jaw action-hero strong. 'You should try it some time.'

'So I should stop rolling around in the shit every day, is that it? If only I'd known. Thanks, GQ.'

'It would be a start,' said Neil. 'You're an ugly fucker, though, so whatever you do, it probably won't make any difference. It's the surgeon for you, mate, I reckon. Something to spend that five grand bonus on that we get for being out here on tour, right?'

Money wasn't the reason Liam had headed back out into Afghanistan so quickly, but it was certainly a perk. Out here, there was nothing to spend your earnings on, so the money just built up in the bank. With a take-home of nineteen hundred pounds a month, and the bounty, as it was generally called, he'd arrive back in the UK with around sixteen thousand quid in the bank. Liam knew that most lads spent that on a car, but he'd not decided himself what to do with his money. Not least because he'd hardly touched what he had from his last tour, and that meant that altogether he'd actually have around thirty grand to play with, more than his parents had ever had in the bank in their whole life.

He stopped thinking about money and focused once more on his arc of fire. 'Is arrogance part of the training for becoming a sniper then, GQ?' he asked.

Neil was the only soldier with them, other than Sergeant Miller, badged as a sniper. And he liked people to know it. Liam didn't mind. As far as he was concerned, if you were good at something, there was no point not being proud of it. And it gave the rest of them a good laugh.

'You have to fill in this checklist before you're even allowed on the course,' said Neil. 'Makes sure only the best get through.'

'And they check if you're good-looking?'

'All kinds of stuff,' said Neil. 'Fitness, brains, how fucking sexy you are. Snipers can't be total heifers, mate.' He tapped, almost affectionately, the scope of his L115A3 rifle. It was one serious weapon. And Neil knew it. 'Imagine some ugly twat like you using one of these? Wouldn't be right, would it? Army knows better than that. It's why they chose me.'

Liam shrugged. 'Mate, I've heard that rifle's so accurate that anyone could use it,' he said, intent only on winding Neil up. 'Even Sunter.'

'You're talking bollocks now,' Neil replied. 'And you know it, you tosser. Sunter's an idiot. Good soldier, but not the brightest, know what I mean?' He tapped the side of his head.

Liam laughed. 'I'm not sure you even know how to use it,' he said. 'For all any of us know, it's an airsoft toy you've had shipped out to big yourself up, make you look cool.'

Neil pulled a spare magazine from a pouch. The rounds were noticeably larger than what Liam was used to, the 5.56 of the SA80. 'See that?' he asked, pointing at a blue dot on the round. 'Snipers get the first five hundred rounds out of the mouldings. Means these are seriously accurate and we don't have to put up with rounds changing trajectory between shots.'

Liam knew that if there was one thing soldiers did well, it was talk about weapons. It wasn't bloodlust or anything weird, they just loved the kit they worked with, and knew it inside and out. A soldier who didn't like weapons was as rare as a rally driver who didn't like cars.

'That's really fascinating,' he said. 'What else can you tell me? It's all so interesting.'

'Fuck off, Scott,' said Neil. 'You just can't handle the fact that when stood next to me I make you look shit.'

Liam laughed and glugged down some water. It was warm: the heat was relentless, even worse in the sangar, and it still felt good. Intensified by the reinforced tin roof and its small size, it was like sitting in an oven and slowly cooking yourself to well done.

Putting the bottle down, he went to stand by the GPMG he was manning and stared out, relaxing his eyes on the middle distance. Carter might have the sexy weapon, he thought, but when it came to sheer firepower, the Gimpy was hard to beat.

Movement.

Liam switched from the GMPG to the range-finder binos. Huge, and so heavy they required a tripod, he stuck his face up against the eyepieces and stared.

'What's up, Scott?' asked Neil, immediately focused. 'See something?'

Liam was quiet for a moment, turning all his attention onto forcing his eyes to pick up any movement, no matter how small.

There it was again.

'Left,' said Liam. 'Five hundred metres. Nine o'clock.'

Judging range was another skill Liam had developed during his time as a soldier. It was a vital skill, allowing a soldier to quickly judge how far away the enemy were and to decide on the best way to engage them, or indeed if engaging was the best option at all.

Neil leaned into his own weapon, eye pressed up against the rubber eyepiece of its impressive sight system.

'Nothing, mate,' he said.

'By that big bush,' said Liam. 'The one with those two trees sticking up out of it like horns. Trust me, I saw something.'

'That's narrowing it down.'

Liam explained further. 'OK, start left, a hundred metres out at the tree stump,' he said, helping Neil track his own weapon out to exactly where he was looking himself. 'Directly above that you'll see a clump of about five or six trees, yes?'

'Eyes on,' said Neil.

'OK, now track up again and move left. Nine o'clock, yeah? See the bush now?'

Neil breathed out slowly. 'On it now,' he said. 'So what did you see?'

'Not sure,' said Liam. 'Might have been nothing. Just want to be sure.'

'What got you spooked then?'

'It's dead out there today,' Liam said. 'Haven't seen a thing. No people, no animals. Then something just caught my eye. Didn't look right. Gut instinct.'

'Right,' said Neil. 'Let's see what we've got then.'

They both fell silent, focusing utterly on what Liam, in a strange way, hoped was something more interesting than a stray goat. Being shot at was no fun, but neither was playing the waiting game and watching animals stroll by as bored as they were. If someone was out there having a nosy, their day, even if only for a few minutes, would get considerably more interesting.

'Got it,' said Neil, not moving from his position.

'What is it?' Liam asked, having spotted a faint movement once again.

'Could be a who rather than a what,' said Neil. 'Need to make sure. You still got eyes on?'

'Yes,' said Liam. 'Can't make it out, though. Whatever or whoever it is, it's well hidden.'

A bright glint of something catching sunlight for the briefest of moments shone out.

Neil came back quick with, 'Did you see that?'

'Yeah,' said Liam, and all his senses were online now as he stared at a possible contact.

'Unless there's a goat out there with binos, then we might have ourselves a dicker,' said Neil.

A dicker was someone working as a forward observer for the Taliban, most probably for a mortar team hidden safely further back in dead ground so they didn't get identified and blown up. Their job was to help the mortar team get their elevation right, reporting back to them on a mobile phone.

'Get Miller,' said Neil, but Liam was already on it. 'If this bastard is about to start bracketing rounds, I'll slot him, but I can't engage without authorization if he's just up there being a tourist and taking holiday snaps.'

'You keep eyes on,' said Liam and pulled away from the binos to shimmy down into the compound from the sangar. Miller was over with the ANA, along with Cowell, Clark and Lieutenant Steers.

It was Cowell who stood and came over to meet him. 'What is it, Scott? Something up?'

'Not sure,' said Liam. 'Might have a dicker. GQ's got eyes on just to make sure.'

Miller and Steers walked over, clearly aware that something was up. Cowell explained what Liam had reported.

'Is there evidence to support engaging?' asked the

lieutenant. 'If it is a dicker for a mortar team, then under Card Alpha we have a strong case for self-defence.'

Liam explained again what he and Neil had spotted. 'Need authorization to engage, sir.'

The lieutenant ordered Miller to put the men on alert, and to get them manning the walls, just in case something did kick off. As Miller did as ordered, the lieutenant turned back to Cowell and Liam.

'Get up there and keep me informed. We need to be absolutely certain this is an imminent threat, and not some whacked-out shepherd. Understand?'

Liam, with Cowell behind, raced back up into the sangar. 'Anything, GQ?'

'Fuck all,' said Neil. 'Whoever or whatever it is hasn't budged.'

'Could be nothing,' said Cowell. 'We need to be sure.'

Neil cut Cowell off. 'Got him!'

Liam pinned himself to the binos. This time, the figure was clearly visible.

'Bastard . . .' muttered Neil.

'What's up?' asked Cowell.

'He's not armed,' said Liam, answering for Neil. 'And if he is spotting for a mortar team, I can't bloody see them.'

'They'll be in safe ground,' said Neil. 'Don't want us

calling in an air strike and ending their fun and games.'

Cowell swore under his breath. 'If he's not armed, we can't engage,' he said. 'We need to link him to an actual threat. You sure there's nothing?'

'He's got binos,' said Neil. 'And he doesn't look like a fucking birdwatcher to me, boss, if you know what I mean.'

'Doesn't matter,' said Cowell. 'We can't risk it.'

'What the fuck is the risk?' asked Neil, irritation in his voice now. 'The only reason any fucker out there is carrying binos is to cop a look-see at us. He's spotting for someone – I know it and you know it. Either that or he's gathering intelligence for a later attack.'

Cowell was quiet, then said, 'What's the distance?'

'Five hundred,' said Liam.

'What about a warning shot, Carter?'

Neil raised his head from his sight. 'You want me to part his hair or just make him dance?'

'Sarcasm is fuck all use out here, Carter,' said Cowell.

'And neither is letting some dicker bastard walk free. It's bollocks, boss.'

Cowell didn't budge. 'I asked you a question, Carter,' he said. 'Under Card Alpha we can use it as a means of escalation. Might force their hand.'

Neil was thoughtful for a moment, then with a slight nod sat back into the sight of his rifle, asking Liam to confirm the distance. For a few seconds, the sangar was silent. The only sounds Liam was aware of was the beat of his own heart, and that of Neil's calm breathing.

The shot rang out and Liam saw, almost instantaneously, a puff of dust kick up at the feet of the person with the binoculars. Neil chambered another round. At the same moment, the telltale dull thud of a mortar being fired punched the air.

'Incoming!' Cowell yelled.

Anyone not on the wall made for cover and an explosion kicked up dust and grit over the back of the compound.

'Missed us,' said Neil.

'Now you can have him,' said Cowell.

'What, not another warning shot? You positive?'

Cowell's stare was enough.

Another thud and Liam knew another mortar round was incoming. It dropped well forward of the compound.

'Next one will be dead on,' said Cowell. 'Take him now, Carter.'

'No problem,' said Neil.

Liam watched Neil. He was calm, motionless, having already adjusted his sight for wind and whatever else a sniper thinks of when doing their job.

The round punched home and the figure was knocked off his feet.

'Shot,' said Liam, but no sooner had the word left his mouth than he saw the dicker rise again.

'Bastard must be wearing body armour,' said Neil. 'That was dead on centre of his chest.'

For some reason, Liam hadn't even considered that the Taliban would be wearing plates under their clothing.

'Where did he get it?'

'Black market,' said Cowell. 'Iran, hard to say. But they're getting their hands on all kinds of kit now. It's a fucking nightmare.'

Neil chambered another round, but as he did so the dicker fell backwards and stumbled off.

When he was gone, Neil said, 'Should've taken him out with that first shot. Now there's a chance this will come back and bite us on the arse.'

'It was the only decision we could make,' said Cowell. 'And you know it. There was no link to a clear threat. Not until that mortar round came in.'

'He was fucking Tally. We all knew it.'

'I'm not saying I disagree,' said Cowell. 'I'm just saying we did it right. You slot some innocent farmer and you'll be up for murder.'

Neil said nothing.

'Anyway, good shooting, Carter,' said Cowell. 'Whoever it was doesn't know how fucking lucky they were to survive that.'

As Cowell exited the sangar, Liam looked back over at Neil. 'I'd put money on us getting no sleep tonight.'

Neil didn't answer. But for Liam, the steely look in his eyes was enough to tell him that he agreed.

It was late evening and Liam was just getting his head down when a shout cracked the night.

'Incoming! RPG! RPG!'

A second later, a dull thud and a flash lit the dark as the shell piled into the reinforced outer wall of the compound.

Grabbing his weapon, Liam raced to the walls as the sound of automatic gunfire detonated from the sangars. Whoever was up there was opening up with the GPMGs.

'Scott!' It was Clint, up on the roof of a room built into the wall. It was used to store food.

Liam ran over and up a makeshift ladder to drop down next to his mate. 'What have we got?'

Muzzle flashes were lighting up the countryside like sparklers, and Liam could hear rounds buzzing past him like wasps. It was a sound that had scared him in the early days of his first tour.

'A fight on our hands, that's what,' said Clint. 'Come on! Move!'

Up at the wall and on one knee, Liam returned fire, Clint alongside him doing the same.

Something detonated about fifty metres out from where they were.

'That was no RPG,' said Liam.

'No,' said Clint. 'Mortar.'

'We were right, then.'

'About what?'

'That dicker that me and GQ spotted,' said Liam. 'The one Cowell had us send in a warning shot first.'

Inside, he knew that he wasn't being exactly fair. X-Factor had done things by the book. But sometimes, Liam knew full well, the best thing to do with the book was to empty a full magazine into it at point blank, and blast the thing to hell.

Another explosion, closer this time.

'Aim's improving,' said Clint.

A bright flash from the sangar closest to Liam and Clint lit the compound.

'Nice one,' said Clint as the rocket from an LASW blasted off through the night. 'Hope it's accurate.'

They both saw an explosion far off, which a moment later grew in violence.

'Direct hit,' said Liam. 'Must've hit the ammo.'

No sooner had he said that than a section of the wall between them and the sangar burst inwards, taking with it two soldiers. The hot air from the blast swept over them, carrying with it a deadly spray of disintegrating rubble. They turned away from it just in time, dropping down behind a section of wall; the stuff rained down about them, smashing and exploding on impact.

Liam didn't need to say anything to Clint. They were up on their feet and over to the damaged section in a flash. It was like a scene from the Blitz, with smoke and burned wood, piles of broken brick and stone, flames.

'Over there!' yelled Liam, pointing to just beyond where the wall had collapsed.

It was Lance Corporal Clark. And he was a mess.

Liam dropped to Clark's side. His mind flashed back to what had happened to his friend Cameron during his last tour, but he pushed the memory away. This wasn't the time or the place.

Clark was unconscious, a wound on his head bleeding red lines across his face, which was ghost white with dust. Whatever else was wrong with him, Liam couldn't at the moment be sure, but the lance corporal's left leg was badly twisted and Liam was pretty sure it was broken. The big Fijian probably had internal injuries too, from the impact of the mortar round.

'Medic!' Nicky dropped down at Liam's side, Cowell with her. 'We need medevac immediately,' she said, getting to work straight away on sorting Clark out. 'I can stabilize as best as I can, but that's about it.'

'I'll call it in,' said Cowell. 'Scott! Eastwood!'

'Boss?'

'See that big hole in the wall?'

Liam nodded. How could they not?

'Don't let any fuckers get to thinking that's a new door, understand me?'

15

It was way past midnight, the dark now giving way to a grey early light the colour of cement. The firefight had died down considerably, with the cover of darkness now on the wane, but it hadn't stopped completely.

A flare, shot up from inside the compound, cracked the sky, lighting up the rough land in front of Liam. And in the odd and eerie flickering light that crept across the desert and scrub like a lost spectre, he was staring hard to get eyes on anything moving towards them. He hadn't seen anything for a while, but they were all still up and ready. It wasn't time to call it a day, not yet.

'Might have to cut my eyelids out in a minute,' said Clint, at Liam's side. 'I'm in serious need of caffeine.'

Following Cowell's order, Liam and Clint had managed to repel all attacks on the hole in the compound wall. They had been joined by a number of ANA soldiers too, including Zaman, and they were both impressed with the way the ANA fought, with ferocious professionalism, their M16s used with deadly accuracy.

Liam rubbed his eyes, blinked hard, told himself he was still awake, didn't need any sleep, not ever.

Movement, far off, but approaching.

'You see that?' Liam asked.

'What?'

Liam directed Clint to where he was looking.

'Can't see anything,' said Clint, staring down his ACOG. 'But in this light it's difficult.'

Liam was sure he'd seen something, kept staring. There it was again! 'You sure you can't see that?'

'I'll keep looking,' said Clint. 'I'll tell you when I do.'

Liam kept his eyes focused on where he'd seen the movement. If it was an animal, it was a big one, and moving towards them slowly, crawling almost.

Zaman drew close. 'What do you see, Scott?'

'Not sure,' he said. 'Eastwood can't see it, but I'm sure I saw something moving, crawling towards us. It's way out, though. I might be just tired.'

Then something was clearly visible and this time Clint saw it too. 'There we are,' he said. 'You were right, mate.'

Liam said, 'What is it? Taliban? He's not moving.'

Clint wasn't sure, said so.

Liam had an idea and turned to Zaman. 'Look,

Shah, you know the Taliban better than any of us. Reckon you could spot one at nearly three hundred metres?'

Zaman nodded. 'Of course. It would be easy.'

Without a second thought, Liam handed Zaman his rifle. Like Clint's, it was fitted with the ACOG, which it had become very clear was the preferred sight for most soldiers out in theatre. 'Use my weapon,' he said. 'Your weapon's accurate, but you've only got iron sights. You'll have a better idea with this.'

Zaman took the SA80 and brought it up into his shoulder. 'Where, Scott? Tell me.'

Liam explained and Zaman moved the weapon until he was dead on.

'Ah, yes,' he said. 'I see him now.'

Liam hesitated, then said, 'Well? What is it? What are they doing?'

Zaman kept the weapon raised. 'I am sure it is Taliban,' he said. 'He is not moving. But he is holding something. A weapon. I am certain of it.'

Liam automatically went through the six-step targeting process in his mind. He took the weapon back from Zaman. 'Thanks,' he said, and got himself into a stable position. Over the PRR he called in to Miller. 'Sarge, I've eyes on a confirmed contact.'

'Clarify,' Miller replied.

'Taliban, two hundred and fifty out, armed.'

'Positive ID?'

'Shah has confirmed also,' said Liam. 'Could be a sniper.'

The sergeant went quiet, but was back on line in seconds. 'You have permission to engage, Scott. Keep me and the lieutenant informed.'

'Boss,' acknowledged Liam, then said to Clint, 'Mate, confirm distance.'

'Two-fifty, hasn't moved,' said Clint. 'And that's definitely a weapon. Shah was right.'

Liam said nothing, settling into the stock of his rifle. The air was dead, no movement. This would be a straight shot. But it was different to a usual firefight. He wasn't hammering rounds into a number of enemy combatants. This time, it was just one and he was being calculated about it, step-by-step.

A shot rang out, but not from Liam. The round thumped home into the brickwork below them.

'Muzzle flash!' Liam hissed.

'Take the shot,' said Clint. 'That first was to get his eye in, check the range for his weapon. He won't miss next time.' He turned to the ANA soldiers. 'Heads down! Now!'

Liam was alone. He held his breath for a couple of seconds, placed his finger on the trigger, breathed out.

Paused . . .

Squeezed the trigger.

The crack of the round leaving Liam's weapon was immediately met by the thud of it hitting its intended target.

Liam immediately followed the shot with another.

'Scott? Kill confirmed?' Miller on the PRR.

Liam called for Clint. They both stared down their ACOGs. No movement. The body was still.

'Target dropped,' said Liam.

A hand rested on his shoulder. It was Zaman. 'That was well done,' he said. 'And you trusted me with your own weapon.'

'Why wouldn't I?'

Zaman said nothing more. Just smiled warmly and gave a nod.

After Liam had taken out the sniper, the Taliban clearly lost the will to fight and backed off. Morning came and everyone was exhausted. But there was no time for resting up.

'Scott?'

Liam was with Clint and Ade helping some ANA soldiers assess and repair the damage to the wall. It was clear that the whole compound needed reinforcing, but other than adding sandbags, there was little they could do.

It would be a patch-up job, which wasn't very reassuring.

Liam turned at his name as Cowell came over.

'Got a minute?'

He followed the corporal.

'Clark was medevac'd back to Camp Bastion,' said Cowell. 'He's doing fine considering, but he's out of action. They're shipping him home.'

Liam was gutted for Clark. He was a good NCO. Didn't shout much, just did the job, was trusted, and also was happy to have a laugh. A good soldier.

'This means,' said Cowell, 'that we're a man down when it comes to responsibility. I need someone to fill Clark's role immediately. And that someone, Scott, is you.'

Liam's mouth dropped open. The way Cowell had spoken, it was almost as though he had sounded out a challenge.

'Catching flies won't help,' he went on, not giving Liam a chance to respond. 'I'm not making you up to lance corporal. This is not a field promotion, understand?'

Liam nodded, still in shock.

'However, you will take on some of what Clark's role involved. So that means you'll be in charge of a fire team, among other things.'

'Why?' Liam asked eventually, his voice unstuck. 'Why me?'

'Don't you want it?'

'That's not what I meant.'

'Good,' said Cowell. 'This is not just down to me, I can assure you of that. Miller and Steers both agree. In fact, it was actually Miller's suggestion. You've the most recent experience out here. You're keen. You've a good working relationship with the ANA and that is vital. Not to mention the fact that you're picking up the language. Oh, and you're a good shot too,' he added. 'Which is why you'll be swapping your SA80 for Clark's weapon.'

'I get the Sharpshooter?'

'Don't get all emotional on me. You're one of the best shots here, we all know it.'

Liam was stunned. After a night of exhausting fighting, he was now being asked to deal with a serious jump in his role. What made it all the more confusing was that it was Cowell delivering the news, someone who didn't seem to like him enough to offer any kind of reward.

'Get your team together immediately,' ordered Cowell. 'We're going out with two fire teams to carry out a battle damage assessment. We need to confirm kills from last night, if possible – not that we'll find any bodies as the Taliban will have taken their dead. But it's good practice.'

Liam knew his one definite kill was still lying out

there. He'd checked later through his ACOG. The body hadn't moved.

'And Scott?'

'Yes, boss?' said Liam.

'Don't fuck this up, understand me? I'll be watching you. Like a fucking hawk.'

Outside the patrol base, Cowell had his fire team, and Liam for the first time had his, making up a patrol of eight men in total. With Cowell commanding, Liam was following his orders to the letter. No mess ups. No mistakes. He wasn't going to give anyone a chance to come back at him saying that he was a bad replacement for Clark.

With Liam were Clint, Ade and James. This wasn't running as a normal patrol, as any contact could be supported easily from the lads up on the walls and in the sangars. So no one was carrying heavy kit, like the light machine gun – LMG – which was based on the Minimi LMG and belt-fed, perfect for sustained suppressive fire. Instead, they were all armed with SA80s, with Clint carrying an under-slung grenade launcher – UGL. James, Liam noticed, though carrying his SA80, also had his combat shotgun strapped to his back. He wondered if James slept with it, as the weapon never seemed far from his side. Liam was armed with his SA80, the

Sharpshooter judged unnecessary for what they were now doing.

After an hour searching, Cowell's voice came over the PRR. 'As I suspected, they've sodded off with the bodies. Anything, Scott?'

Liam was making his way over to where he'd taken out the sniper. 'No bodies,' he replied. 'Plenty of blood splatter, though. Looks like some of them got really fucked up. It's a mess in places.'

'They pick a fight with us,' said Cowell, 'then they can expect nothing less.'

Liam had his three move forward. 'Cowboy? Can you see it yet?'

'Nothing,' said Clint. 'You sure it's this way?'

Liam was positive they should've been on top of his kill. He'd done his best to memorize the very spot he'd dropped him.

Then a shout. 'Hold!' It was James. 'Up ahead, Scott. Direct. Body on the ground. Partly hidden.'

Liam looked, spotted it. 'Nicely done, Stirling,' he said. 'I'll go check it out.'

'No you won't,' said James. 'I will.'

Liam glanced round at him. Was he disobeying an order? Trouble was, Liam wasn't sure he'd given an order in the first place. He'd just said he was going to check on the body. *Shit*, he thought, *this is my first time out as a fire team commander and I'm already fucking it up.*

Liam said, 'What's up, Stirling? You see something I can't?'

'Not yet,' said James. 'But I'm used to spotting stuff you wouldn't see till you stepped on it and it took your legs off at the knees. I'll go check first.'

Liam was impressed. James was putting himself on point because his skills matched the need at that moment.

James slipped forward. Liam kept an eye on him, had Clint and Ade scan the scrub around them, ready and alert.

James came back.

'Well?'

'Fucker's booby-trapped,' said James.

Liam wasn't sure what he was getting at. 'How do you mean?'

'The body's wired up to something I can't see,' James replied. 'Someone must have sneaked in, set the body up, then legged it. Crafty bastard.'

Liam was taken aback, not just by what James had discovered, but by the fact that his actions had potentially saved his life.

He called it in over the PRR. 'We'll need Shah out here,' he said. 'He's best placed to deal with this.'

'That decision is not yours to make,' Cowell replied.

'Fall back to the compound. We'll discuss there.'

'But, Corporal—' began Liam, but Cowell cut him off.

Back in the compound, Liam was with Cowell, Miller and Steers.

'We should send Shah,' Liam said again. 'Stirling says the body is fitted up with some kind of explosive device. He couldn't see it but he was pretty sure.'

'My view is we call it in, sir,' said Cowell. 'We need the lads from Bastion out here. Counter IED. They're best suited for this.'

Lieutenant Steers thought for a moment, then said, 'I think Corporal Cowell has a point, Scott. Shah is good, I agree, but none of us have seen him deal with this kind of situation. He may have no experience.'

Liam noticed that Cowell was staring at him, almost daring him to disagree.

'Yes, sir,' said Liam. 'Shall I punch it through?'

'Yes,' said Steers. 'Is the site marked?'

Liam nodded. James had marked the body and surrounding scrub with almost a whole can of the red spray paint he used to identify possible IEDs.

'Then call it in now.'

Liam set off to where the radio was situated when Cowell came over. 'A word to the wise,' he said. 'It's never a good idea to openly question someone senior. Me, or the lieutenant.'

'I wasn't, I didn't . . .' said Liam.

'I'm just telling you now,' replied Cowell. 'You may be good, but don't get cocky. If you do, I'll be all over you, Scott, of that you can be certain.'

Cowell turned and left Liam alone to punch in a call to Bastion. As he did so, he reflected on what had happened. How had he been cocky? He wasn't even sure that he had. But Cowell probably had a point, he realized. He was now more visible to the corporal, and to Miller and Steers. His actions would be scrutinized very closely. He needed to be even more alert.

Mistakes were not an option.

16

A few days later, Liam and the rest of the multiple, with Zaman along on Lieutenant Steers's request, had left the compound to head on out to the next ANA patrol base, PB2. The first month in Afghanistan was already over and for Liam it had flown by. The pace of what they'd been doing hadn't let up from the moment they'd got off the plane. From the RSOI training in Bastion, to the firefight on arriving at the HLS, and on through everything since, Liam hadn't had a chance to sit and think about what he was doing. Not that it mattered. He was happy to be soldiering, and to be doing it with a bunch of blokes he trusted.

He sometimes found himself thinking about Martin, but because he had already gone through the loss of Cameron, he felt better equipped to deal with his death and it wasn't affecting him like he'd initially worried it might. And now, with Lance Corporal Clark gone, he was responsible for his own fire team, and had been given charge of Clark's Sharpshooter rifle, in addition to his own personal SA80. Life was tough, but it was that which kept Liam hooked. He was learning all the time, even by his mistakes.

'Another day, another shit hole,' said Rob, dropping his bergen off by a bed in PB2.

'Look, if you're not happy with the accommodation, you should talk to the manager,' said Clint. 'Ask for an upgrade.'

Rob wasn't listening, though. Once again, he was back on his iPod.

Zaman came over. 'Corporal Cowell has asked for you,' he said to Liam, and pointed across the compound. 'Over there.'

'What's it about this time?' Liam asked.

Zaman shrugged. 'He did not say. I was told to get you. That is all.'

Ade sparked up with, 'Off you go, then. Remember to take an apple for teacher.'

'Piss off,' Liam replied. 'I'm not his pet.'

Ade laughed. 'Denial won't work, Scott,' he said. 'The more you deny it, the more it becomes obvious that it's true. Now be a good boy and fuck off.'

Liam tried to laugh it off, but couldn't. Now that he'd been given additional responsibility, Cowell seemed to have made it his mission to be on him 24/7, making sure he was keeping an eye on things, giving him additional responsibilities like carrying out spot checks on weapons and feet. The weapons Liam didn't mind, but checking people's feet was not his idea of fun. It made sense, because if your feet were shagged, you were useless out on patrol. He'd managed to delegate the role to Nicky – she was the medic, so it made sense – but he still had to be alongside. Well-cared-for everyone's feet may have been, but sweet-smelling they weren't.

Liam walked over to Cowell. 'You wanted me, boss?'

The corporal motioned for him to sit down. 'We'll be running a patrol later,' he said. 'We're doing a recce into a potentially hazardous area.'

'How so?' asked Liam.

'As you know, Yakchal is a proper badlands place. Highway One is the focus of the ANA. They work in the main on keeping it clean, keeping it secure.'

'It's the main supply route through the area,' said Liam. 'They've not got much choice.'

'Exactly,' said Cowell. 'Which is why they want us to have a scout about to see if the Taliban are around and up to some of their shitty bollocks mischief.'

'They have suspicion?'

Cowell nodded. 'They've got intelligence, but it's scant, to say the least. All they really know is a whole stack of mights and possibles. We need to see if any of that has the potential to become definites.'

'So what's the plan?'

'We're going for a look-see,' said Cowell. 'Get an idea of the area, use binos to get a wider idea without treading too far into what could be a big pile of shit.'

'Why not use the trucks?'

Cowell shook his head. 'They'd draw too much attention,' he said. 'We'll be able to get enough of an idea with this approach. We'll see what to do after. Right?'

'I'll get everyone together,' said Liam. 'What time are we going?'

Cowell checked his watch. 'Get everyone to push their scoff into their faces. We'll go at 1300.'

It was just gone two hours into the patrol and Zaman, to everyone's frustration, was dealing with the third IED that day.

'Not liking this,' said Ade. 'Area should be clear. It's like someone's got their eye on us, putting sodding IEDs down ahead of us every step we take.'

Liam was inclined to agree, and again found himself thinking back to when they'd come under sustained attack on arrival at Patrol Base 1. But he kept those thoughts to himself; no point spooking everyone even more than they probably already were.

'Just keep your ground sight working,' he said, knowing that despite his reservations, which were growing with every step, it was Corporal Cowell's call. IEDs or not, the patrol was going ahead. And with James on point and doing a good job of finding them, and Zaman dealing with them in his usual relaxed manner, Liam wasn't too worried. Not yet, anyway.

'I've not blinked since we set out,' said Clint.

Zaman came past, the IED now safe. Liam nodded a thanks.

'An easy one,' said Zaman with a shrug. 'Could do it blindfolded.'

'I'd prefer it if you didn't,' said Liam.

Zaman grinned and walked on past.

'Still can't believe he doesn't wear protective kit,' said Rob. 'Fucking mental. One of those things go off, at the range he's at, all we'll get to see is pink mist and no more Shah. The lunatic.'

'He's good,' said Liam. 'That's what counts. And if he thinks wearing that stuff will hinder him, then I'm not going to complain. Whatever it is he does, it works.'

Nods all round. Everyone agreed. They'd all grown to like Zaman, and it hadn't taken long for the soldiers to accept him. He was easy-going, which helped, as did his sense of humour. But above all, he'd done a good job in keeping them alive, never bragging or expecting thanks, just getting on with it and doing it well.

An hour later, Cowell called Liam up over the PRR. Liam headed up the line to chat face-to-face.

'We've scanned this whole area,' Cowell said, pointing at a map in his hands. 'I've enough notes from what we've seen to put a report together for the ANA on potential Taliban threat. Do you have anything to add?'

Liam shook his head. 'I've given you everything we've all seen,' he said. 'The Taliban are here, I'm sure – the IEDs are evidence of that – but wherever they are, they're hiding well.'

'Could be caves,' said Cowell. 'The ANA have mentioned that the area round here has pockets of them. Not that they've checked them out.'

'Can't blame them,' said Liam. 'We all know what happened in the caves of Tora Bora.'

During the second Iraq war, the SAS had gone into a warren of caves occupied by the Taliban and Al Qaeda. The fight had been close quarter and brutal, the SAS troopers in the end resorting to hand-to-hand, falling back on using knives. Caves were not a good place to go pick a fight. Despite that, though, the SAS had come out on top. It was already told as legend.

'Don't worry,' said Cowell, 'we're not about to go looking. That's the job of the sneaky beaky lads, the ones doing reconnaissance stuff. SAS, Pathfinders, Recce Platoon.'

Before joining the army, Liam's view of the blokes who passed SAS Selection was that they were untouchably hard. You just didn't fuck with the SAS. Since joining up, he'd learned a little more about them, and the rest of the lads doing reconnaissance. They weren't built like Superman, and most of their actual role was to collect intelligence deep behind enemy lines. What made them hard was that if anything kicked off, they were usually left to their own devices to get the hell out. Their motto wasn't just 'who dares wins', it was: *train hard, fight easy; train easy, die*. And a small part of Liam, the part that had kept him going through his training, stopped him giving up, wondered if he too had the steel to pass and join such an elite group.

'So we head back?' he asked.

Cowell nodded. 'I'll bring up the rear this time,' he said. 'You can lead us back in.'

Liam nodded confidently, but underneath his gut was twisting. This was another step up in what he was having to do. He just had to focus and everything would be fine. With Cowell watching, hawk-eyed and seemingly keen for him to make a mistake, he had no other choice.

* * *

The walk back to the compound was quiet, really no different to the walk out. The scenery was the same, the sun, moving slowly across the sky, burning down on them with the same heat. Liam spotted things he'd seen on the way out, odd rocks here and there, a bush he remembered for no real reason. But – and why it was he couldn't quite pin down – every step had him spooked. Something was up, but he didn't know what. Everything looked normal, but his sixth sense was going haywire.

Half an hour into the walk back, James pulled everyone up.

'Got another one,' he said to Liam over the PRR.

'But we cleared the way,' said Liam, and his sense that something was wrong was immediately heightened. 'This is ground we've already walked. You positive?'

'I fucking know that,' said James, an edge to his voice. 'This one is right where we walked. It's even got our footprints over the top of it.'

Liam went cold. Someone was out here with them, following, and with lethal intent.

'Say again?'

'This one is right under our route out here,' said James. 'I shit you not, Scott. Some fucker's sorted an IED under our feet.'

Liam called for Zaman and explained.

'Very dangerous,' said Zaman.

'It's an IED,' said Liam. 'Of course it's dangerous.'

Zaman shook his head. 'No, that is not what I meant, Scott. Listen . . .'

Liam leaned in closer.

'It is not as you may think with IEDs,' said Zaman. 'They are not laid and set to detonate at the same time. The Taliban are sneakier than that.'

'How do you mean?'

'They lay the IEDs first,' said Zaman. 'They can leave them there for months if they wish.'

'Why?'

'They wait,' Zaman continued. 'They wait for soldiers to be in the area, then they go round and connect up the battery packs. This means all evidence of digging is gone.'

'So what you're saying is someone's come back and connected this one up because we've been pinged? They've been watching us?'

Zaman nodded. 'This, and others perhaps. I do not know. But this one for sure.'

'Shit . . .'

'Scott, what's the hold-up?' Cowell was on the PRR. 'Why is Shah talking to you when he should be up sorting the IED?'

Liam fed back what Zaman had told him. 'They're

following us, boss. Probably have been since we left. I don't like it.'

'And neither do I,' said Cowell. 'We need to shift. And by shift, I mean get a fucking move on!'

Liam ordered Zaman forward. But no sooner had the ANA soldier dealt with the IED than the telltale crack of gunfire shattered the moment and dust was kicked up all around the patrol.

Liam registered immediately where the incoming rounds were coming from and directed his fire team accordingly. Clint unleashed a hellish rate of fire with the LMG.

'Sunter?' Liam ordered over the PRR.

'Yes, boss?'

'Muzzle flashes at two hundred. Grenades! Now!'

Ade's SA80 was fitted with the UGL. And on Liam's order he dropped in three grenades with pinpoint accuracy.

'Scott!' Cowell's voice came in over the radio. 'We need to get the fuck out, now! Is that IED clear?'

Liam looked up, saw Zaman, who gave him a thumbs up. James was with him. 'Yes.'

'Then move out! Go!'

Liam made ready to give the order, but at that moment two successive explosions went off at close range. Not close enough to kill, but close enough to kick dirt and grit over everyone around him and fill the air with thick dust.

Liam blinked the stuff away, his eyes stinging. Standing up he grabbed Ade by the shoulder. 'We're moving! Now!' He called over to Clint, 'Keep their heads down for a few seconds, then get the fuck out!'

'I'm on your heels, mate!' Clint called back.

Liam raced ahead, looking for cover. And not just a bush either, but something that had a chance at stopping a round coming in, like an old log or a mound of dirt, anything. Trouble was, he was trying to find something while on the move, whereas whoever was shooting at them had been there long enough to make sure they were well hidden. Another explosion, closer this time, and he jumped sideways, rolled along the ground, and was up again on his knees. Then, a few metres ahead, through the dust and smoke, he saw a shadow. At first he thought it was one of the lads, but the silhouette was wrong: no kit, no weapon, and definitely not in combat kit. Whoever it was, they were on the ground messing with something. Not actually by the track either, but at its side and down a shallow gully.

Liam crept forward, ignoring the pain in his knees and elbows as grit and stone dug in. As yet, he couldn't see clearly enough to either identify the threat, or fire. He had to be sure.

Crawling further, and still unnoticed, the sound of the battle around him disguising his own movement, he was now only metres away, the dust in the air still doing its best to hide him from view. Then a faint gust of wind caught the grubby air, twisted it into swirls, and it cleared.

For the briefest of moments, the man glared at Liam with undisguised hatred. Liam stared back hard and cold. There was something familiar about the figure, something he recognized, but he couldn't place it. Kneeling on the ground, he was wearing the usual Afghani dress of dark baggy clothing, over which was a battered combat jacket. His face was half hidden with beard and the shadow from the cloth hat on his head, and his hands were still, frozen in the task of attaching wires to a small pack covered in plastic. Liam knew in an instant: the man was Taliban, and he was connecting a battery to an already long-buried IED, just like Zaman had described.

Liam already had his weapon in the shoulder and saw that the figure was unarmed. It was all the hesitation his enemy needed.

With a raging bellow, the man leaped at Liam. Caught off guard, Liam struggled to stay balanced, rolling as the man grabbed his weapon. Liam didn't let go, brought a boot up into the man's stomach and hammered hard, then again. It made no difference. Liam had heard that some of the Taliban got high on drugs before heading off to fight. It was just his luck to find himself up against one such fighter, he reckoned.

He rolled again, kicked his assailant where it hurt the most, sending him spinning. But the force of it hooked his rifle out of his hands. The man was on his feet, didn't give Liam time to breathe. Liam dodged, got to his own feet, tried to remember some of what Clint had shown him, went for his sidearm, but the man was into him too quick. And he wasn't coming in with fists, but rocks.

Liam blocked the hits, but he was caught and knocked to the ground. Dazed, he managed to dodge another attack. Then finally, as the Taliban fighter yelled out and came in for more, Liam managed to draw his sidearm and fire.

The first shot did nothing. The second slowed him. The third and fourth dropped him to his knees. The fifth hit him in his right cheek, collapsing the side of his face, then took off the back of his skull.

Liam was exhausted and holstered his pistol. He'd used it in anger before, and it was different to letting rip with an SA80. With an assault rifle, the target was usually at a distance. With a pistol, the fight was close, you saw the person you were aiming to kill eye-to-eye. But now wasn't the time for quiet reflection. That would come later, if at all. Grabbing his rifle, Liam went back to his fire team.

'Where did you go?' asked Clint, who had moved position, but was again laying down suppressing fire. Tim was there as well, returning fire efficiently, but almost as though he was alone, thought Liam, like the rest of the patrol didn't exist.

'Found someone connecting an IED,' said Liam, breathing hard.

'Put up a fight, did he?'

Liam nodded. 'Fucking understatement. He was wired on something himself, I'm sure of it. Took five shots to drop the bastard.'

Cowell called over the PRR. 'They're backing off,' he said. 'No more waiting around. Let's shift it!'

The patrol moved then, as though they were all running to a pre-programmed set of orders. Executing perfect fire and manoeuvre drill, they were soon back at the patrol base, albeit on their chin straps and close to puking with exhaustion.

'Here.'

Liam looked up and saw fresh water. It was Miller, who'd come to meet them as they arrived. Liam sipped carefully, so as to avoid the stuff hitting his stomach and coming straight back out again.

'Thanks,' he said, handing the bottle back. The rest of the lads were grabbing a drink now too. Tim, though, had for whatever reason moved away from the others. He had issues, Liam thought, but so long as he got on with the job, then he wasn't too bothered. It didn't help though if someone saw themselves as different to the rest, an outsider.

Miller spoke. 'You all look fucked,' he said. 'What happened?'

Liam explained, and as he did so, realized something. 'The bloke I shot? He was from the village we visited weeks back.'

'You sure?'

'Positive,' said Liam. 'Came with an old guy with a bad leg. I thought he was a shifty bastard when we met him. Turns out I was right.'

Steers came over. 'This doesn't sound random,' he said. 'Not from what you and the rest of the lads are saying.'

Liam looked up at the lieutenant. 'You mean it was planned? They knew we were coming?'

'I'm not saying anything yet,' said the lieutenant. 'But the only people who knew we were heading out are within these walls. To get wind of you turning up, and to arrive with sufficient numbers to cut you off and try to block your exit with pre-laid IEDs – that takes planning. Serious, fucking planning.'

It was the first time Liam had heard the lieutenant swear. It added a certain gravitas to the situation, as though everything that had happened up to this point had been just bad, but this was seriously messed up. Liam was also aware that what the lieutenant had said was right in line with what Rob had voiced after the Chinook was hit. Was there really an insider threat?

'But who would do that?' he asked, not wishing to make a big deal out of his own thoughts on it quite yet. And anyway, he had no evidence, nothing additional that would help the situation.

Steers said nothing, but his eyes strayed over to the ANA, and in their sweep took in Zaman.

'No way, sir,' said Liam. 'Shah's golden, all the lads trust him.'

'It's none of our boys, clearly,' said Steers. 'It has to be local intelligence. It's the only answer.

'We need to find out how this information was leaked,' he went on. 'And Scott, you're our main contact.'

Liam shook his head. 'Shah is with us,' he said. 'Trust me.'

'I do trust you,' said Steers. 'But I also have to uncover exactly what's going on here. And I need your help to do that. No argument. Understand?'

'Sir,' said Liam.

The lieutenant left and walked over to the rest of the patrol.

Later, when everyone had calmed down, and the patrol had been fully debriefed, Liam was having a lie-down and trying to work out exactly how he was going to help the lieutenant. All he could really do, he realized, was just keep his eyes and ears open. Not only were they out in the wilds with the Taliban clearly up for a fight, they had someone in the patrol base who was happy to betray them. He remembered Zaman saying his brother was in the Taliban. But would he really be stupid enough to say that, make himself number one suspect, then go off and direct fire? Liam wasn't convinced. It didn't make sense. But he still had to follow orders.

'Oi! Scott! What do you think?'

Clint interrupted his train of thought. Liam glanced up and grinned at what he saw.

'GQ got his bird to send them over,' said Clint. 'Brilliant!'

Clint, much to Liam's and everyone else's amusement, was now sitting on his bed, feet pushed into a pair of bright red grandad slippers, and puffing away on a pipe.

'Not one for smoking, I have to say,' said Clint, 'but this pipe rocks!'

Liam laughed. He'd heard that the post had come through, but he'd not had time to check if there was anything for him. He wasn't expecting anything – there was no one really back home to send it.

'Suits you,' he said. 'You our grandad now, then?'

'Fucking old enough,' said Ade. 'But that pipe does smell fit. What baccy is in it?'

Clint lifted up a metal tin. 'Says here it's something called Sunset Breeze.'

'Better than those fags you chuff on, Sunter,' said Liam.

'Makes me look wise,' said Clint, then laughed. 'Not sure the wife'll agree, though!'

After the firefight they'd just survived, it was a much-needed release to be joking around. And the arrival of post was always a welcome distraction.

'There's something on your bed,' said Clint, pointing.

Liam was surprised. He walked over and picked up parcel. Inside was a note: 'Hello, chap! Sorry it took so long to get these printed. Good memories! Regards, Chris.' Behind the note was a pack of photographs. Liam slipped them out and laughed.

'What's so funny?' asked Clint. 'It can't be me. I look awesome.'

Liam handed the photographs over one at a time, the first showing him, Chris and Jason, pint glasses in hand, each of them wearing a sombrero – Jason's idea of livening things up a bit.

'It's the reason I'm here really,' he said with a laugh. 'Took a holiday, found I missed being out in Afghanistan!'

Liam's laugh was cut in half as a shout bounced across from the other side of the compound. Liam turned to see James backed into a corner, hands up in defence.

And in front of him, fists up and ready, was Tim Harding, closing in for a kill.

17

Liam was up and across the compound in a shot.

'Harding! Stand down, mate! The fuck are you doing? Stand down!'

Tim wasn't listening, his eyes focused on James and nothing else.

Cowell turned up. 'What's going on, Scott?'

'Don't know, boss,' said Liam. 'Stirling?'

With Tim holding off, James said, 'Don't ask me, Scott. All I know is, we've come off that bitch of a patrol and this loon decides to have a go.'

'There's more to this than that,' said Cowell, and moved to step between James and Tim.

'Don't! Just fucking don't!' Tim yelled. 'This bastard called me a coward, that's what happened! A coward, you hear? And I'm not a fucking coward! I'm not!'

Liam looked across to James, raised an eyebrow. 'Really?'

James shook his head. 'He was saying he wasn't going out again,' he said. 'Started mouthing off that what we're doing is pointless and that he wasn't doing it any more. All I said was that we don't give up on a job we're here to do. That's what I said.'

'I'm not a coward!'

'I didn't fucking say that!'

Tim edged forward and James looked at Liam and Cowell. 'Seriously, if he gets any closer I'm going to nut the mad bastard, so someone better stop him.'

Liam could tell that James was holding himself back, doing the sensible thing and trying to keep the situation as calm as he could. But it looked like Tim wasn't listening and Liam had a sense that, were it to kick off, James wouldn't hold back.

'Harding, you need to calm down. No one has called you a coward. Whatever this is about, we can talk about it.'

Cowell came in. 'Scott's right. Calm down and back away. Nobody wants to see us fighting each other. That's not why we're here.'

For a moment, it looked like Tim was listening. Then, without warning, he lunged at James.

James was ready for it. He dodged right, let Tim fall past him, then had his hands up, ready for a scrap. And, Liam noticed, it looked like he knew what he was doing, a boxer's stance.

Liam didn't give it a chance to get to that. He jumped in, pushed James away, then grabbed Tim.

'Hold off,' he shouted as Tim struggled. 'Just calm the fuck down.'

Tim lashed out, his elbow slamming into Liam's face. His nose took the brunt of it, and he fell back, but he didn't let go, not even when he felt blood dripping into his mouth.

Cowell jumped in and at last they managed to pin Tim to the ground.

Lieutenant Steers jogged over. 'I'm assuming there's an explanation?'

James gave a quick run-down of what had happened.

'Right,' said Steers. 'Stirling, I want you over at your bed to calm down. Corporal, bring Harding to me – we need to talk this through. Scott, get yourself to Harper – you're bleeding. And no arguments from anyone. Just do as ordered.'

That done, Steers turned on his heel and strode off, clearly angered by what he'd just witnessed. Liam couldn't blame him. It was stressful enough without in-fighting.

Liam found Nicky.

'Just for the record,' she said, 'I'm not here just to keep you looking pretty. What happened?'

Liam explained. 'Harding's clearly gone a bit wrong,'

he said. 'I've been watching him and he's never seemed totally relaxed. Now this. Mental.'

'Stress out here affects everyone differently,' said Nicky, taking a closer look at Liam's nose. 'Does it hurt?'

'Of course it hurts!' he said. 'The twat elbowed me in the face!'

Nicky reached up to touch it. Liam flinched. 'Look, I need to see if it's broken or not. And I can't really do that just by looking.' Liam held still and Nicky gently checked his nose. 'Well, I don't think it's broken,' she said. 'He just caught you hard, that's all. The bleeding is already stopping anyway. Here.' She handed him some tissue and he held it to his nose. 'Don't put your head back. That does nothing. You just have to let it bleed out and clot naturally. It won't take long.'

'Your bedside manner sucks,' said Liam.

'You should see me on a bad day.'

Liam made his way back to Clint and the others. 'Don't ask,' he said.

'So what was all that about with Harding and Stirling?' Clint asked.

Liam sat down. 'Not sure,' he said. 'Steers and Cowell are with Harding now. He's not seemed relaxed or right since we arrived, if you ask me.'

'What makes you say that?'

'Not sure really,' said Liam. 'But he's not got the

attitude right. I mean, it's crap out here, but we chose it, right? No point beefing on about it. Get the job done, stay alive, look out for your mates, get home. Harding, though – he just always seemed on edge, in a bad way.'

Liam heard his name called out. It was X-Factor.

'No rest in this place, is there?' he said, making to leave.

'This is the army, mate,' said Clint. 'And you know you love it.'

Liam found Cowell sitting with Steers and Miller. 'Where's Harding?' he asked.

'Calming down,' said the lieutenant. 'We need to decide what to do. And quickly.' He added, 'Scott, he's refusing to fight. I'll leave it at that. I could go on and give you every reason he gave us, but it's not important. The fact of the matter is, we now have a soldier who is refusing to do what he's paid for.'

'And that's a problem,' said Steers.

'Then he's putting all of us at risk,' said Liam, still holding tissues to his nose. 'If he's not out with us, we're a man down, and that means less firepower, less protection.'

'I agree,' said Miller. 'But we can't force him out on patrol either. He'd be even more dangerous out with us in this state of mind. No telling what he'd do. For all we know he could run off or turn the weapon on himself or us.'

'So what are our options?' asked Liam, suddenly struck by the fact that he was now fully involved in a discussion with the leadership of their multiple, and they wanted his opinion.

'We have to keep him here till we can get him back to Camp Bastion,' said the lieutenant.

'Swap for a replacement?' said Liam. 'Will there be one? Most soldiers are out on jobs. We can't exactly nab someone from another multiple.'

'Indeed,' said the lieutenant. 'Regardless of that, we have to keep him here for the now.'

'So we keep him busy then,' said Liam, growing in confidence. 'There's plenty to do here. We can have him sorting kit, keeping the place tidy, working the cookhouse. We can't have him sitting around.'

'Explain why not,' Miller said, his voice hard.

'Because it'll shag everyone else's morale,' said Liam. 'Harding decides he doesn't want to play any more and gets to just sit on his arse? Fuck that, boss. He's paid to be here, and if he doesn't want to be out where it's dangerous, then he can bloody well make himself useful.'

He saw a grin crack Miller's face. 'You sound pissed off,' the sergeant said.

'He nearly broke my sodding nose,' said Liam. 'So yeah, I'm pissed off.'

'Then how's about you run him?' said Miller. 'Keep him busy, occupied, and out of the way of everyone else, while we do our best to get him out of our hair.'

'No problem,' said Liam, looking at his blood-soaked tissues. 'No problem at all.'

With his nose finally no longer bleeding, Liam had Tim working right away. His temper had calmed, but it didn't change the fact that Tim was a part of a team and, regardless of his views, had a role to play. So he set him up with a duty rota and got him working. That done, he gathered the rest of the lads together and explained what was going on.

'So he's fully weapons down?' said Ade. 'What an absolute twat.'

Liam nodded. 'So it's like I said, we have a choice: force him to come out on patrol with us, or have him be useful here.'

'It's a no-brainer,' said James. 'He's flipped. I wouldn't trust him with a fucking water pistol, never mind an assault rifle.' He tapped his head and everyone agreed.

'But what I don't want,' said Liam, 'is any of us making the situation worse, OK? That's not going to help anyone. Yeah, we're all pissed at him, but this is the best way to manage it.'

'Don't know what you mean,' said Rob.

'Yes, you fucking well do, Hammond,' said Liam. 'No winding him up. No pranks. No taking the piss. If Harding's got issues, then that's his business. Out here, what we do can take its toll. If we leave him be, and he's kept busy, everything will run smoothly. None of us want morale to take a kick in the balls too. Right?'

Everyone nodded an agreement.

'You know what, Scott?' said Clint. 'You're sounding like a proper NCO. You'll be on the NCO course when we get back, I'd put money on it.'

'Ha-bloody-ha,' said Liam.

'It's a compliment,' said Clint. 'You're doing a good job.'

Two days later, Liam was again called over to a meeting with Cowell and Miller. Lieutenant Steers was busy meeting with the ANA and everyone was impressed not only with his leadership, but with how he'd developed their working relationships with the ANA. It was in no small part down to his own belief in what they were doing, and his drive to ensure it was done properly, that everything was going as well as it was. Liam found Cowell and Miller leaning over a makeshift table that was covered in maps. Empty mugs were scattered around, one of which was stuffed with wrappers from the chocolate bars they got sent through from home.

'How's Harding doing?' Miller asked without looking up, his eyes following a line traced by the index finger of his left hand across one of the maps.

'Fine,' said Liam. 'Busy. The lads are keeping cool too, even telling him he's doing a top job when they see him.'

'Great,' said Miller. 'Job done.'

'So what's this about then?' Liam asked. 'Because I'm guessing it's not about Harding.'

'We've had some intelligence from the ANA,' said Cowell. 'Possible weapons cache. Sounds like it could be a major kick in the teeth for the Taliban if we find it.'

'You're assuming the intelligence is sound,' said Liam. 'We found nothing at that village back at PB One.'

'That was more a case of keeping your eyes open just in case,' said Cowell. 'This is something else entirely.'

'We've had your mate Shah confirm the source,' said Miller, finally looking up at Liam, his expression all frown and little else, 'So we think it's good. We have no cause to think any different, do we, Scott?'

Liam was pleased to hear confidence in Zaman, but he still wasn't sure. 'I know it's been quiet this past couple of days, but that patrol when we got seriously screwed over still bothers me.'

'How so?' asked Cowell. 'You've found no evidence of anyone acting for the Taliban and neither have we, right? Looks like they were just there at the right or wrong time, depending on how you see it.'

Liam shook his head. 'They knew we were there,' he said. 'Must've been watching us to sort IEDs for when we headed back over the same ground. That's not happened before.'

'The Taliban are a capable force,' said Cowell. 'We can't ever underestimate them.'

'My gut still tells me something's up,' said Liam. 'We were hammered as soon as we arrived out of Bastion, like they knew we were coming. This is a major step-up in their aggression towards our presence here. We need to be cautious.'

Cowell's reply was sharp. 'Well, we can't exactly rely on your gut, can we, Scott?' he said. 'Remember, this is down to Miller, me and Steers. Not people going on their feelings, or the rub of a lucky rabbit's foot.'

'But what if it's a trap?' said Liam, thinking out loud now. 'What if this is all just a way to get us out to somewhere the Taliban are waiting for us?'

'It isn't,' said Cowell, certainty in his voice. 'The ANA have already done a recce of the area. It's clean. There's no sign of the Taliban being active. All we need to do is go in, check, and if the weapons are there, bring them back. If not, we're still win-win, because we've acted accordingly and in the process ensured another area is being patrolled, shown face to the Taliban to let them know they don't run this, not any more.'

Liam knew he was getting nowhere. Cowell wanted the weapons cache and that was clearly what they were going to be doing, no matter what the possible risk.

'Could we not send a small team out first?' he asked. 'A four-man recce?'

'Like I said,' Cowell said, 'the ANA have already been up there. It's unnecessary.'

What Liam wanted to say then was: what if someone in the ANA wasn't playing by the rules? But he knew Cowell wouldn't listen. His mind was made up.

'When are we going?' he asked.

'Tomorrow, first thing,' said Miller. 'Get your fire team ready. Briefing at 1700. Make sure everyone has at least a good attempt at some kip tonight so we're fit to go in the morning.'

Later, with his fire team giving the weapons a thorough service, cleaning everything to a shine, oiling where necessary and checking and rechecking every working part their lives depended on, Liam grabbed a moment with a brew. He still wasn't happy about what they were doing, but he knew Cowell wasn't going to listen. The best he could do was have his fire team prepped and working well. He knew he could depend on them, but he didn't want them sent on a wild-goose chase. Worse, he didn't want them walking into an ambush.

Sipping his tea, Liam sensed someone was close by.

'Fire team sorted?'

It was Cowell. When wasn't it? thought Liam. The man seemed to be almost omnipresent.

He nodded, said nothing.

Cowell sat down. 'What you need to realize, Scott,' he said, 'is that if we do find a serious weapons cache, we'll be saving lives. Not just one or two, but potentially hundreds.'

'I know that,' said Liam, aware now that his voice wasn't exactly calm. 'I'm just not convinced. What if there's more to this than we know? What if the only thing waiting for us is loaded weapons in the hands of a bunch of Tally waiting for us to walk right up to them like we actually want to be shot?'

'It's not your decision.'

'Never said it was.'

Cowell stood. 'Not everything we do out here has to be guts and glory,' he said.

'I'm not saying that either,' said Liam, annoyed that Cowell would even suggest such a thing. 'In fact, I never have.'

Cowell leaned in. 'You've had your moment, kid,' he said, a sneer licking the edges of his words. 'We all know it. But don't let that go to your head. Know what I mean?'

'I didn't ask for the medal, if that's what you're getting at,' said Liam, angered now and confused by the sudden attack.

'Just remember your place, Scott. You're a soldier, and soldiers take orders.'

'You talk about medals,' said Liam, struggling to keep his voice down, 'and it sounds to me like you want one yourself, only you want it for not even pulling the bloody trigger!'

'Well, I'd rather have one for that than for getting my mate's foot blown off!'

Liam's blood boiled over. Corporal or not, Cowell was bang out of line now and was in line for a swift kick in the teeth.

'You absolute fucking bastard! That's not what happened and you know it!'

Liam had never spoken to Cowell about what happened during his last tour, but he knew that most of the lads around him had heard what had happened. It was all part of being awarded a medal. He'd never bragged about it, but people had asked and he'd told them, simple as that. Word got around, as it always did. And the memory of being chased by the Taliban, fearing for his life like never before, was still raw and haunting.

'Just do your job, Scott, understand?'

Words failed Liam, and he had a job holding back the urge to slam into Cowell and kick the living shit out of him.

The corporal said nothing more and walked off, leaving Liam alone wrestling with his barely suppressed rage. When he eventually calmed down, and headed back to check on his fire team, he made a mental note to keep an eye on X-Factor. He'd done a great impression so far of being a good corporal, but Liam knew deep down that something wasn't right, not least because of Cowell's lack of combat experience.

But then again, he wasn't the only one Liam was wary of. Something was up – he just wasn't sure what.

18

'Is it me, or is it seriously quiet?'

Clint's question caught Liam off guard. The previous night had been a restless one. He'd woken numerous times, his brain refusing to stop chewing over what Cowell had said. His gut was twisting itself into knots a sailor would be proud of.

'Early morning,' said Liam. 'It's always quiet.'

'I guess,' said Clint.

Liam attempted a relaxed smile. Around him, the rest of the patrol was doing a final weapons check. The day itself looked like it was setting itself up to be a good one. It was bright, golden almost, and a light breeze was doing just enough to take the edge off the oven-like heat. A part of Liam wondered what Afghanistan would be like without all the conflict it had suffered, still was suffering. But it was going to be a long, long time before it ended up as a holiday destination.

'How's the pipe and slippers?'

'Magic!' said Clint. 'Soon as we get home, I'm getting myself down to this little tobacconist's I know of. I tell you, pipes is where it's at!'

'Bit too Bilbo Baggins for me,' said Liam.

A few minutes later Cowell ordered the patrol out of the compound. Despite the usual army practice of rotating the lead scout, James had insisted on being on point, with the combat metal detector already sweeping left and right, and his matt-black shotgun slung by his side.

Clint, Rob and Ade – Liam's fire team – walked ahead of him, and he couldn't help but feel proud to be not only fighting alongside them, but leading them too. However, he was still unable to shift the niggling sense that none of this was right. What Clint had said about the morning being more quiet than usual now seemed more ominous. Perhaps he was making it up, but as they walked further away from the relative safety of the compound, it really did seem quiet. Not that the area around them was always abuzz with noise, but there was a definite eeriness that Liam couldn't explain, almost as though every bush and scrub was waiting for something to happen, the very ground – if it could do such a thing – holding its breath.

Half an hour into the patrol, with everyone stopped

for a water break as Cowell checked their route, Liam noted something else and mentioned it to Clint.

'Never been this long without Stirling finding or spotting something,' he said.

They were stopped on a slight rise, a large rock- and boulder-strewn valley spreading beneath them. It was a barren place, with faint patches of scrub dotted here and there like the first signs of measles on skin, a rash that grew more obvious the closer to the valley floor you looked.

'Must be a good sign,' said Clint. 'Perhaps the Taliban have finally realized they've lost and bugged out.'

Liam wasn't so sure, but neither was he happy to say any more. He didn't want to get the folk around him spooked. However, he also had a job to do and that meant ensuring everyone was on their toes.

'Make sure you all keep an eye out for anything that doesn't look right,' he said as they made to move out again, a wind picking up for the first time since they'd set off. 'This may be going nice and smoothly, but I don't want us getting complacent. Right?'

It was a further thirty minutes before they arrived at their destination, about halfway down the valley, the ground flat and wide and unwelcoming, Cowell bringing the patrol to a stop.

With each footstep Liam's sense of foreboding had

grown. He'd done his best to ignore it, tell himself it was just his mind paying too much attention to things that probably weren't important, but he still couldn't shake it. And worst of all, he couldn't shake the ominous sense that they were being watched. Not that he'd seen or noticed any evidence to suggest it; in fact quite the opposite: the patrol had been running smooth and unhindered. It didn't matter, though; he was sure something was up. He was also sure that mentioning it to Cowell was pointless – unless he wanted his ears chewed off again, that was.

'Scott?' It was Cowell and he was waving for Liam to join him.

He walked up to the front. 'Is this it?'

Cowell showed Liam the map. 'We're here,' he said, his finger on a section of the map that to someone who couldn't read the landscape looked no different to any other bit of it. 'And the weapons are, we hope, over here.'

His finger moved a little, and Liam looked up to where Cowell was indicating. It was about a hundred metres further on, an area of relatively flat ground, its only real defining feature that it seemed strangely bereft of the larger rocks and boulders that were scattered everywhere else.

'I want Stirling to check the area first,' said Cowell,

'then you and I will go back with him for a look-see.'

'What are we trying to find exactly?' asked Liam.

'From what we understand, it's a covered scrape,' said Cowell. 'All we can do is look and keep our fingers crossed.'

Liam nodded and surveyed the area ahead, then scanned the ground immediately surrounding it, his eyes then slipping up the valley sides. Was it an ambush? Was it all a trick? Again, there were no signs of any such thing, and the patrol had so far gone off without a hitch. He still didn't like it, though, and as James walked off he headed back to check on his fire team.

'Keep your eyes scanning everywhere,' he said, now more keen to have everyone alert than to keep his suspicions to himself.

'Something up?' asked Clint.

'It's like you said before we set off,' said Liam, 'it's quiet. And when Stirling gets back and I'm heading up there with Cowell, just stay alert, right?'

Back with Cowell, Liam watched James come back towards them.

'Nothing,' he said. 'Place looks clean.'

'Completely?' asked Liam.

'A few fresh animal tracks,' said James, 'but nothing else.'

'Come on, then,' said Cowell, and Liam couldn't miss

the edge of excitement to his voice. 'Let's go see what we've got . . .'

Liam let Cowell take the lead. Not that he had much choice, as Cowell strode off ahead. However, as they edged closer to where the weapons were supposedly hidden, he let James past again to make sure everything was safe.

Walking away from the patrol, Liam found himself becoming increasingly aware of each footfall, each breath. The smallest of sounds were seemingly growing with the distance between him and the others. Shadows cast by plant and rock looked oddly darker, and even the sun seemed to burn hotter.

'I think I've found it!'

Cowell's excited voice pulled Liam out of his thoughts and he was pleased about that. He wanted to find the weapons and get back to the compound. Hanging around where they now were had him spooked and he didn't like it. His soldier's sixth sense was off the scale.

He moved forward to stand with James and Cowell. 'Where? What?'

Cowell pointed. 'That large boulder to our left? The one that's triangular in shape?'

Liam spotted it right away.

'That pyramid one?' asked James.

'That's what I was told to look for,' explained Cowell. 'That's where the weapons are.'

When they reached the rock, Liam couldn't see anything that suggested anything was hidden anywhere. Then his eye caught an odd line in the ground. It was straight and ran for about a metre. The only reason he spotted it was because it had been hidden in the shadow cast by the pyramid rock.

Liam called James, and pointed at the line in the ground. James stepped carefully towards it. All of a sudden, he yelled as the ground gave way beneath him and he dropped to his knees.

Liam raced over.

'I'm OK,' said James. 'Look – wooden planks. Rotted to fuck.' He cleared away the dirt in front of him to reveal the old bits of wood.

Cowell came over. 'This is it!' he said. 'We've found it!'

James lifted himself out of the hole and they all looked down into it.

It was Liam who spoke first. 'You see what I see?' he asked.

'What's that?' asked Cowell.

'Fuck all,' said Liam with a sigh. 'Absolutely fuck all.'

* * *

'So you think they grabbed the stuff before we arrived?' asked Liam.

They were back with the rest of the patrol and deciding what to do next. The hole under the planks was empty except for a few spent shells. The whole thing had been a ghost chase.

'That hole was fucking ancient,' said Cowell, and Liam heard the venom in his voice. 'Hadn't been used in months, probably years. Fucking intelligence was bollocks . . .'

'Then let's just get back,' said Liam. 'I don't like us being out here thinking that someone possibly wanted us here in the first place, if you know what I mean.'

Cowell's eyes were dark. 'Ambush?'

'You said it, not me,' replied Liam. 'But we were sent out here for a reason, and I'm guessing that reason isn't just to have a laugh at our expense, is it?'

Cowell glanced back to where the weapons were supposed to have been hidden. Liam did the same, then scanned back, looking again for any sign of movement, any hint that they were about to have a contact.

'Agreed,' said Cowell, 'Right, Scott, get back with your fire team. We're heading back. But keep your senses keen. Some fucker sent us out here and for all we know they're watching.'

Liam was back with Clint and the others. 'We're heading back,' he explained. 'There's a big fuck-off hole, but no weapons. Hasn't been used in ages.'

'How do you know weapons were ever there at all?' asked Rob. 'Could be just a big hole that we should drop X-Factor in for wasting our time.'

Liam understood Rob's sentiment. They were all pissed off about heading out and finding nothing.

'The place is clean except for a few shells and a dead spider,' he said. 'That's it.'

'So what now?' Clint asked. 'We just head back?'

Liam looked at the three blokes with him. He trusted them, had seen them fight, knew they were solid. 'That's the plan,' he said. 'Any thoughts?'

'About what?' asked Ade. 'That we've found nothing, or that we've come out here in the first place after some bollocks intelligence?'

'Both,' said Liam.

Clint spoke with lowered tones, calm, but serious. 'Doesn't make sense,' he said. 'Why would anyone send us here for no reason?'

'That's what's bothering me,' said Liam.

'If it's an ambush, why hasn't it kicked off already?' questioned Rob.

Cowell came over with his fire team. Liam couldn't

help notice how even out here Neil looked cool, like he was half expecting some paparazzi to pop up for a few candid snaps.

'Ready?' he asked.

'Yes,' said Liam.

'Then let's get back,' said Cowell. 'I don't like this. Stirling – on point. Everyone stay alert. Let's move!'

19

About thirty minutes into the hike back, Clint called over his PRR, 'Movement. Right. Five hundred. Two o'clock.'

Cowell brought the patrol to a dead stop. 'Scott? Get your scope on that now.'

'Already on it,' said Liam, his weapon – the Sharpshooter – already raised and in his shoulder. Slowly he scanned the area as Clint directed him to where he'd seen movement. 'What was it? Anything specific?'

'Wind's moving everything that way,' said Clint, pointing his hand forward, 'but whatever's out there was pushing grass the opposite way.'

'Can't see anything.'

Liam kept his weapon in the shoulder, forcing himself to examine every bit of ground he could.

Then the crack of a rifle split the air. The sound was immediately followed by Clint falling to the ground.

Everyone had seen the muzzle flash. And it hadn't come from where Clint had seen movement.

'Return fire!' yelled Cowell. 'Fucking have it!'

Liam dropped down next to Clint, scared shitless of what he was going to find as the rest of the patrol opened up on where the muzzle flash had come from.

Clint groaned as Liam did a quick check, but he could see no obvious entry wound, no blood. 'You're OK,' he said. 'Don't ask me how, but you are.'

Clint sat up and as he did so Liam saw a hole in his helmet.

'Christ . . .' he said. 'Your helmet . . .'

'What?' asked Clint.

'You have a guardian angel?' asked Liam.

'Not that I know of.'

'Well, the hole in your helmet says different,' said Liam. 'The bastard got you, but your kit did its job and kept your head on your shoulders. Close call, mate. Nearly shat myself when you dropped.'

'Was like someone smashed me in the skull with a cricket bat,' said Clint, already pushing up and getting his weapon, the LMG, ready to return fire.

'I think we've got a sniper,' said Liam. 'Where you saw movement, that wasn't where the shot came from. The fucker moved.'

Clint was up. 'Suppressing fire, Eastwood!' Cowell

called over the PRR. 'Scott, we need to get out before that bastard takes another pot shot! Carter?'

'Boss?'

'Stop worrying about your hair and slot that bastard!'

'On it.'

Clint opened fire. Liam saw Neil run for cover, then his rifle was out and he was scanning for the target.

'Fire and manoeuvre,' Cowell ordered. 'In twos. Shift it!'

With Clint keeping the sniper's head down, everyone started to move off. Liam stayed with Clint.

'You see anything?'

'Nothing,' said Clint. 'But he's probably keeping his head down with all this flying at him.'

Liam wasn't convinced. 'Keep firing,' he said. 'I'm going to slip back the way we came, try to get eyes on. I'll be right after. Carter?'

'Haven't got a clean shot.'

'Stay there. I'm heading round, see if I can close in. If you have a shot, take it.'

Clint kept on with the LMG, the rest of the patrol moving out in twos.

Liam scanned the horizon. The first movement had been at two o'clock, but the muzzle flash of the round that had kicked Clint off his feet had come from further round at four.

Slowly, and keeping very low, Liam slipped back the way they had come, this time making sure to put to good use any cover he could find. Just ahead he spotted an old tree stump hidden by scrub and he settled in behind it.

Liam kept calm. It would probably come to nothing, but something was telling him the sniper was moving in behind them to take them out as they retreated back to the compound.

He lay there for a minute, watched as Clint took a final burst, then was up and off. Then, further round but still a way off, he saw something: grass moving against the wind rather than with it, just as Clint had described before. Liam brought the Sharpshooter to his shoulder, levelled the sights on what he'd seen. At first it was just grass, probably an animal. Then he saw something that didn't fit in with the surroundings, something long, thin and straight. It was what you were always looking out for, telltale signs of unnatural forms, and nature didn't do stuff in straight lines. It had to be the barrel of a rifle.

Liam flicked off the safety, waited.

Behind the barrel, the person holding it came into view. He was crawling forward, slowly, surely, confidently. Liam was reminded of the last time he'd done this, back in the compound after the wall had been blown apart. That shot had been just over two hundred metres. This one, if he took it, was well over five hundred. It wouldn't just be testing his own skills, but the capabilities of the weapons system he was now handling.

He took a breath, took another, calmed himself as he brought the crosshairs of the sight down onto the sniper. It was then, as he was about to take the shot, that he realized something: the sniper wasn't aiming at the patrol, the bastard was aiming at him!

Liam dropped as the report of the sniper's weapon cracked the silence and the round hammered into the front of the tree stump. The energy of it rippled through the old wood, sending splinters skywards.

Fuck it, thought Liam, *he's after me now*. He scanned around for other cover, knowing that to stay where he was would be asking to be shot. There was a shallow ditch about twenty metres away. It was a sprint, but he could make it.

Liam gritted his teeth, rolled to his knees, head down, then bounced up, hammering his legs like he was trying to crack the ground with every step.

Another shot rang out. Liam saw it kick dirt up just ahead of him. He skidded into the ditch then crawled away from where he'd landed.

Everything was quiet. Now Liam had a choice – run to catch up with the patrol and risk getting shot, or take the sniper on? He slipped up the side of the ditch, keeping himself hidden behind a small bush, and allowed his eyes to get used to what they were seeing, which to begin with wasn't much. But he quickly identified where the sniper had been when he'd taken the shot. He didn't expect him to be still there, so he tracked down, then found him. And he was moving fast.

Liam brought his weapon up again, zoned in on the movement in the grass that was betraying the sniper's path. He couldn't take a shot until he had a clear line of sight. He didn't want to risk giving himself away. This one had to count. And he knew that it was him or the other guy, simple as that.

The sniper stopped. Liam saw the weapon brought round. He again eased off the safety. There, filling his sight, was the distant image of the person who'd taken a shot at Clint and was now trying to kill him. They were both staring at each other down their weapons across a distance of at least five hundred metres.

Liam took the shot.

All he saw was the weapon drop suddenly; that was it. He kept his sights on the sniper, chambered another round.

The sniper moved, weapon up again, a shot rang out, clipping the edge of the ditch less than a metre away from where Liam was laid up.

He didn't flinch, took another shot, and this time he saw the sniper's head snap back and the rifle fall. Head shot. And there was no getting up from that.

Liam was on his PRR to Cowell. 'Sniper down,' he said. 'Where are you? And where's Carter?'

'I'm here,' Neil said, over the PRR. 'Awesome shot, Scott. I'll follow you in.'

'We're two hundred metres on,' said Cowell. 'We'll cover both of you, just in case. Move it!'

Liam heard gunfire and was up and sprinting, heart pounding, not just from exertion, but from what had just happened. Neil was close behind. He'd won in the end, come out alive, but he was fully aware of just how close he'd been to finishing his tour with a round in his head.

Back at the compound, everyone was quiet. Liam was cleaning the Sharpshooter rifle. He wanted the weapon spotless.

'We've done a battle damage assessment,' said Miller, coming over to Liam. 'No body, but we found blood and shells. It was a hell of a shot. Even Carter was impressed, and that's saying something. The cocky bastard is sometimes just a little bit too self-assured.'

'The sniper nearly got me first,' said Liam.

'He didn't, though,' said Miller, then sat down. 'What about the cache?'

'What about it?'

'Thoughts?'

Liam sat back, his weapon neatly laid out in pieces on a canvas sheet on his bed.

'I think we're lucky to have got back,' he said. 'I don't think it was supposed to be a lone sniper.'

'Is that your gut speaking again?'

Liam smiled a little. 'Doesn't matter,' he said. 'We were sent out there on crap intelligence. That's the issue that's bothering me.'

'My point exactly,' said Miller. 'Cowell's questioning Shah right now.'

Liam snapped up at this.

'Shah? What the hell for? It's not him, if that's what you're thinking.'

'He confirmed the source,' said Miller. 'What do you know about him? Really?'

Liam remembered what Zaman had said about his brother being in the Taliban and didn't want to say.

'Look, if you know something that is important, you need to tell me. Think, Scott. This is about the safety of everyone here. We need facts. It's not escaped anyone's attention that, with all the stuff that's been going on since we arrived, it's like someone's been one step ahead of us all the way.'

Liam sighed. He didn't want to suggest anything

about Zaman, not least because he was sure he could be trusted, but neither could he keep what he knew to himself.

'He has a brother,' he said. 'Only whereas Shah is ANA, his brother is Taliban.' Then he added, 'It's common practice apparently, the family just making sure all bases are covered.'

Miller nodded thoughtfully. 'Yeah, I've heard that happens,' he said. 'But it does put a different slant on things, doesn't it?' He got up. 'Well done today,' he said. 'Tomorrow we've another patrol with the ANA. It's our final one here before we bug out to the next PB, so we need it to be smooth and by the letter, understand?'

'Boss,' nodded Liam.

'And we'll all be keeping an eye on Shah,' Miller said; then he was gone.

Picking up the barrel of the Sharpshooter, ready to start clipping the weapon back together, Liam thought about what had happened that day, and about Zaman. Was he really behind it? Had he been party to them being led into a trap that, in the end, could have been a lot worse?

That night, for the second time in forty-eight hours, he hardly slept.

* * *

'Shah, you're with me,' said Liam, as the patrol made ready to leave.

Zaman smiled at Liam. 'It is a bright day today,' he said. 'I heard about what happened yesterday on the patrol. I am glad you are safe.'

Liam had no idea what to say. He didn't know if Zaman was being genuine, or if he was behind what had happened in the first place. Was he now staring into the face of a man who, behind the smiles and the friendship, had been party to Liam nearly getting killed? It didn't seem possible, but what had happened over the last two days had got everyone spooked.

'Me too,' said Liam.

Clint was next to him. 'What about the Sharpshooter?' he said. 'You're not taking it with you?'

'The Sharpshooter is all very well,' said Liam, 'but to be honest I'm more comfortable with my SA80. And it's better for close quarter.' The weapon, thanks to its bullpup design – with the magazine behind the pistol grip – was unobstructive and quick to bring onto a target.

Cowell pulled everyone together, his and Liam's fire teams making up their patrol, with Zaman walking with them, alongside the four-man ANA patrol, which would be taking point. Nicky was also tagging along as the patrol was skipping past an occupied compound. If anyone was home, it had been decided a friendly medical drop-by would be a good thing to do, and would help them leave the area on a positive.

'This is our last walkabout,' the corporal said. 'Let's keep ourselves alert and ready. We don't want any fuck-ups. Smooth, people, understand?'

Everyone nodded.

'Right, then let's move out.'

An hour or so later, Liam, with his fire team all walking in line in front of Cowell's group, and the ANA patrol up ahead, was already looking forward to the patrol being over. It was cloudier than usual, and a cool breeze was blowing. He could sense that everyone was getting itchy to turn round and head back. Liam felt the same; after what had happened the day before, they were all wondering if someone was out there right now, just waiting for a signal.

About three hundred metres ahead was the compound Nicky was along to visit. It was the only building in the area around them, the rest given over to gullies and bush, rising up behind the compound to a horizon that drew a faint line across the mountains in the distance. The only clear signs that it was the home of a family somehow managing to scrape a life from the rough ground around them were the three goats tethered outside and a small pile of metal cooking pans.

Clint said, 'You know what, Scott? I can almost taste the brew waiting for us. Hot tea on a hot day: you can't beat it.'

'A bottle of ice-cold beer gets pretty close,' said Liam.

'Cider,' said Clint. 'None of that gassy rubbish either. I'm talking proper stuff. Get it seriously cold, have one on a hot day, and you're singing!'

'Please don't sing,' said Liam. 'You're not exactly Julie Andrews.'

'Voice of an angel, actually,' said Clint. 'Used to be in the church choir.'

Liam laughed out loud. 'You do talk some bollocks.'

'The trouble is,' said Clint, 'it's all true. Every single word.'

An explosion cut the conversation dead.

'IED!' Liam called across the PRR, all his senses coming on line, sweeping the area around them for any sign of attack. 'Man down!'

He wasn't in charge, Cowell was, but he had responsibility for his fire team and their safety and that of the rest of the patrol.

Liam grabbed Nicky and ran down the line. What met them was a mess. The ANA point man, who was doing James's job today, was unconscious, and considering what had happened to him, Liam knew that was probably best. From what he could see, both legs were smashed to pieces and the blast had ripped up into his chest and face. Blood was everywhere, mixed with muck and dirt and grit.

Miller and Cowell took control, directing everyone into fire position, ready for attack.

Liam and Nicky approached the injured man. 'Shit . . .' It was even worse close up. The soldier's legs weren't just smashed, but gone at the knee, with flesh and bone and blood covering an area of about three metres. The V of the explosion had continued its violence further up, taking an arm off just below the shoulder, and peppering his body with fragments of metal and dirt and stone. Liam had seen this before, when his mate Cameron had died on him during his last tour.

'Keep your head together,' said Nicky, dropping down at the man's side. 'We need medevac immediately.'

Liam grabbed the radio off Ade and called it in. Then the world came apart at the seams as a storm of rounds came in at them from all sides.

Ambush . . .

20

'Cowboy – keep those bastards' heads down!' Liam yelled out over the crack of weapons all around them. 'Sunter, Stirling – back him up. Anything that moves, shoot it!'

Liam was in full control of his fire team. Trouble was, rounds were coming in from all directions, it seemed, a full hundred-and-eighty-degree arc in front of them. And at its centre, the compound. It was definitely still occupied, though clearly now by the Taliban and not the family they'd hoped to visit.

As yet, the ground behind them, the route back to the compound, was clear, but Liam wondered how long it would be before they were completely cut off.

He called over to Ade, 'Grenades! Drop a few on them. That should keep them from thinking this is going to be a walk over. Then move left – *cover*!'

They'd just passed through a dip in the ground, and

the area had around it a few low bushes and fallen trees. It wasn't much, but it would do.

Ade loaded the UGL, aimed, pulled the trigger. The grenade bounced out of the small metal tube slung under his SA80 and a moment later crashed down into the compound. The explosion was followed quickly by two more as Ade sent a volley of three, then four grenades into them. One fell short, another blew a hole in the wall, and the final two landed inside, sending up faint mushroom clouds of dust.

As Liam had ordered, everyone found cover behind scrub, and were up and firing. Ade had his weapon in his shoulder and was returning fire. James was next to him and they worked smoothly together, providing fire, then covering the other to change magazines. Training was taking over. Everything they were doing was automatic. The situation may have been frightening, but Liam knew he was at least fighting with the best, and that was something he knew he could depend on.

'Scott?' Miller on the PRR.

'Boss?'

'You got eyes on anything? Contacts? Numbers?'

Liam scanned around, trying his best to see what they were dealing with. But there was so much coming in at them it was almost impossible to estimate. And they had no way of knowing just how many Taliban were still alive in the compound after Ade's volley of grenades.

'All I can see is one big shit storm,' he yelled, directing as best he could his team's rate of fire. 'From what we've got coming in at us, we're talking heavy numbers. At least twenty or thirty fighters.'

He wanted to be more accurate, but it was impossible. All he knew was that they were outnumbered. That didn't mean all hope was lost, because Liam knew that numbers didn't count for much if the enemy were using knackered weapons and firing indiscriminately. And he knew he was part of the best fighting force in the world, well trained, motivated and used to working as a team – all factors that gave them a much better chance, not only at getting out of there alive, but also at giving the Taliban a fight they'd not forget in a long, long time. But being outnumbered did mean the job of getting out would be a whole lot harder.

'Then they *knew* we were coming,' said Miller. 'You don't get this many Tally just turning up for a scrap unless they know something. And we need to break out before this is a total cluster fuck.'

Liam scanned where muzzle flash was seen. It was nearer than before. Shit . . . the bastards were moving in. Not just from the front either, but edging round their left and right flanks.

'Boss, I think they're trying to cut us off! They're

closing in on us. If we're not careful we'll be overrun!'

The implications of that happening were too awful to imagine. Liam knew that when pushed, most of his lads would say they'd rather die fighting than end up in the hands of the Taliban and in front of a movie camera.

'You on that radio?'

'Calling it in now!' yelled Liam, with Ade next to him, returning fire.

'This is a troops-in-contact situation, Scott,' said Miller. 'We need air support. Fast!'

Troops-in-contact meant that they had no organic means of getting themselves out of danger. In other words, they couldn't do it alone. The words were chilling to hear and Liam gritted his teeth; they were going to have to fight with everything they had to get out of this alive.

One of Cowell's fire team was up with a LASW. The rocket shot out across the field of fire and into an area of brush out of which the heaviest fire had been coming. The rocket dug into the position and detonated, destroying everything within blast range. The firing stopped. But elsewhere it just upped in tempo.

Liam ducked instinctively at the sound of a round zipping past him. Then Ade snapped backwards, hammering into him, knocking him down, pulling the radio away.

'Sunter!' Liam rolled Ade off his legs. He was hit, blood pooling out from a thigh wound. 'Harper! Man down!'

Nicky was in fast. 'The point man is KIA,' she said to Liam. 'I'm sorry. We couldn't save him.' She turned to Ade. 'Sunter? Sunter! Listen to me! It's Harper!'

Shit, thought Liam, one killed in action already. They needed to do something to turn this fight round, but what?

Ade was yelling through gritted teeth. Liam thought about the ANA lad, blown apart by an IED. This patrol was going from bad to completely screwed in short order.

Nicky cut open Ade's combats where the round had hit him. Liam saw blood and little else, then Nicky washed it with water and he saw the wound, a rip torn across Ade's flesh.

'It's a flesh wound,' Nicky said. 'It's not serious. He'll be fine. I can patch it up here, then clean it properly when we get back. We need to move!'

Another shout came back, this time from the ANA soldiers. Another man down.

'We're getting torn apart!' Liam hissed down his PRR.

'Focus, Scott!' Miller said, coming back. 'This has only just started.'

Nicky patched a field dressing over Ade's wound. 'It'll hurt, but you'll be fine. Can you move?'

'Pass me my weapon, Scott,' Ade hissed.

'I said you could move, not fight,' said Nicky.

'Bollocks to that,' said Ade. 'Weapon, now.'

'You're injured,' said Liam.

'No, mate,' said Ade through gritted teeth. 'I'm seriously fucking pissed, is what I am!'

Liam handed Ade his SA80. He was returning fire immediately. Liam could see Taliban falling, as muzzle flash went skyward or just bounced backwards, but they were always replaced by another fighter. How many of them were there?

Liam was back on the radio, called it in, giving the coordinates of the compound.

'They're right on top of us,' he added. 'Take out the compound but nothing else or we'll be hit too.'

Liam looked up – the Taliban were even closer now: a hundred metres, if that. They were still taking fire from the compound, but if the Taliban on the ground got closer, any further air support would be completely useless.

The call ended. Miller was next to him.

'Well?'

'A quick reaction force have already left, and Apache are scrambled,' said Liam. 'A fast jet is going to deal with the compound. But we need to make distance or we'll be too close for them to take a shot. Can't risk blue-on-blue.'

Miller ordered everyone to fall back and the order was followed immediately, with everyone working their best to cover each other as they made to retreat, fire and manoeuvre all the way, back down the route they'd walked out on. Ade was partly supported by Nicky so that he could make the distance with them.

The sound of a jet cut through the air. Then it was gone, and the compound disintegrated as the bomb shattered it – and anyone inside – into a million pieces.

But there was no time to celebrate as Liam heard gunfire from the direction they'd just come from. Quickly, he directed Clint to return fire.

'I hate to say this, boss,' Clint said, 'but I think more are joining in. They're getting reinforcements.'

They were already twenty minutes into the firefight, with one ANA KIA, and two injured, though Ade was seemingly oblivious to what had happened to his leg.

'We've only got so much ammunition,' said Miller. 'We can't just sit here spitting fire at them till we run low, then run out!'

Another rocket blasted out, taking out a further

Taliban position. They were repelling with everything they had, but the Taliban were still advancing.

Liam glanced up and down the line. Everyone was returning fire, steely-eyed, jaws hard, making good use of any cover available, be it a tree or a rock. Then he spotted someone slipping away from their position. It was one of the ANA soldiers. He was making a break for it, but he didn't look scared.

Liam's world stalled. Was this the traitor? The man who had been feeding intelligence to the Taliban? What other reason would there be for leaving the fight? He certainly wasn't just running because he didn't want to die – he was heading off because he knew what was going on.

Liam felt fury rising inside him. It was because of this man's actions that Mascot had died, that his ANA point man had been killed, that they were in this shit storm now. He shouted out, but the soldier wasn't listening. He tried again, but still the Afghan kept moving.

'Cowell!' he bellowed, pointing towards the man.

Cowell was closest to the soldier but hadn't noticed the man's actions. The corporal turned and followed Liam's line of sight, saw the soldier trying to slide away and moved towards him, ready to drag him back. But as he drew close, the soldier turned and opened fire and Cowell dropped backwards into the dirt.

The soldier then turned his weapon towards Liam, but he didn't get a chance to squeeze the trigger, as Liam and Miller opened fire simultaneously. The soldier was dead before he hit the ground.

'That'll be the bastard who was leaking information then,' said Liam.

Miller nodded. 'Yesterday was probably just to see if we'd take the bait. Having us patrol that area gave his mates a chance to get dug in here without us noticing.'

'Well, the fucker's dead now!' Liam said grimly.

Rounds came in and they both ducked. Liam made to go check the ANA soldier over and see about Cowell.

'I'll do that,' shouted Miller. 'You stay here. Keep on them – don't let them close in any further or we'll be dancing with them, OK, Scott?'

Liam saw Cowell sit up as the sergeant approached. The corporal was alive, probably down to the ANA being a crap shot and shooting from the hip, and his body armour doing its job.

But as Miller helped Cowell, he went down hard too!

Liam knew then what else they were dealing with. 'We've a sniper out there too!' he shouted. 'Cowell and Miller are both down!' He glanced across at them. Nicky had already crawled over there and they were both moving, so that was something.

Liam pulled himself back into the fight. The Taliban

were even closer now. The jet had done what it could, but if the Apache arrived, it would be unable to help: the Taliban were too close. He quickly radioed in their current situation. The message was relayed to the pilots to hold off until further orders.

An RPG raced overhead, slamming into the ground behind them, covering them with dirt. Ade dropped the bloke in a breath. Liam sighted another RPG being made ready.

'Ade! Left, two hundred, ten o'clock!'

Ade swung his weapon round, fired. The fighter holding the RPG fell on his face, trigger depressed. The rocket bucked out of the tube, but instead of zipping over into Liam and his fire team, it dropped way short and into a group of Taliban. The explosion tore them to pieces.

'We can't just sit here!' Clint yelled. 'I'm down to my last fifty links. I've my SA80, but I've been passing my mags around. Ade's running low. We all are!'

'Grenades?'

'All spent,' said James. 'We're all down to our last. Then it'll be sidearms. We need to do something now to turn this round, or—'

James stopped speaking. What he was about to say they all knew didn't need to be said. Getting captured by the Taliban was something they all knew was a risk, but it was the most horrifying prospect they could imagine. So they weren't even going to entertain it.

Liam suddenly noticed something. 'It's gone quiet,' he said. The silence was eerie, doubly so after the relentless sound of gunfire. 'I don't like it,' he added. 'How close are they?'

'Close enough to spit at, pretty much,' said Ade. 'Thirty metres, max. What are you thinking?'

A single shot rang out. It was still enough to make them jump, keep everyone down.

'I'm thinking we're in a heap of shit and they're just waiting for us to run out of ammo. They think they've already won.'

'What if they've bugged out?' said James.

Liam had a look, and a round ploughed into the ground in front of him.

'They're still there,' he said.

Everyone fell quiet. Liam looked back at Cowell and Miller. They were both still in the care of Nicky. Neither looked fit to fight.

At last, Liam spoke. 'The only way out of this is to scare those fuckers into realizing just what a bunch of hard bastards we are.'

'What are you thinking?' asked Clint.

'Bayonets,' said Liam. 'We charge them!'

21

'You're absolutely fucking insane, Scott!' said Ade. 'A bayonet charge? This isn't the trenches! We're not in World War One!'

Liam held a hand up to quieten him down. Shots were still coming in.

'They're closing in,' he said. 'We all know it. And they're too close for the Apache to do anything without killing us in the process.'

'Are they here yet?' asked James.

Liam said, 'They're holding off until we've made distance, then they'll hammer them. They can't do anything until then. There's a quick reaction force on its way too, but that'll take longer and could be too late.'

'And until then?' said Clint.

'The way I see it,' said Liam, 'is that the Taliban have been running this fight since it started. We need to take control. If we overrun them first, we can turn this.'

Meeting with silence, Liam called over the ANA officer to hear his plan. Two minutes later, it was agreed.

The SA80 would only take a bayonet if the UGL wasn't fitted. Because of this, Liam had Ade bin his own and swap it for Miller's weapon. Clint took Cowell's. Finally, the remaining rounds were shared out equally.

'We go on my mark,' said Liam to the rest of the patrol. 'Eastwood, when I say, you empty the LMG into the Taliban line. The ANA lad with the PKM will do the same. That'll keep their heads down. We then lob in every last smoke grenade we've got. Then, when I say, we up and charge and we keep firing all the way.'

'What would the corporal pricks back at Catterick say?' asked Ade. 'Firing while on the move? Breaking the rules, mate. Fucking right we are!'

'They won't be able to look up and see us until it's too late. By that time we'll be into them or they'll be dead.'

'Or we will,' said James.

Everyone fell quiet.

Liam was alone with his thoughts for a moment. He knew that the effectiveness of the bayonet charge wasn't so much about the possible close-quarter fight with bayonets. That was part of it, and they'd all had their training, but no one really wanted to get that close and personal, close enough to smell the breath of the enemy as you ram a shard of metal into their gut.

As a weapon, the bayonet itself was rugged and simple, the hollow handle slipping over the barrel of the SA80 and clipping in place. The bayonet charge itself was more about terror. It was a scare tactic, and a terrifying one at that, its only aim to crush the enemy with fear at the sight of men bearing down on them, bayonets fixed, yelling and screaming for blood.

It was soldiering as tough and terrifying as it could ever get.

And it was what they were about to do.

The silence seemed to thicken, as though the stress and fear of the moment were leaching into the air around them, sending it sour.

Liam relieved his bayonet scabbard of the deadly and silent weapon it contained. Autopilot took over and the bayonet was attached before he'd even realized. He glanced around, knew everyone was in that same frame of mind, just letting the training take over, doing the job, dealing with the fear, the sickness rising in the stomach to be pushed down.

Now everyone was just on their PRR, waiting for the word. Liam took a breath, held it, then released.

'Eastwood! Now!'

Clint and the ANA soldier both opened up on the Taliban line. The ground was peppered with rounds. A few tracers from the ANA soldier's weapon set some of the dry grass alight and soon small fires were burning, sending wisps of smoke into the air.

'Grenades!'

On Liam's call, four arms launched canisters into the air, trailing grey smoke behind them. Landing, the smoke thickened and soon the whole area in front of them was gone, lost to the fog from the grenades.

This is it, thought Liam. *This is fucking it . . .*

He was on his feet. 'Move it! Come on! *MOVE!*'

As one, the soldiers were on their feet and charging, sprinting across the ground. Clint, the LMG spent, was up with his own SA80. The ANA lads were alongside, all of them raging, all of them charging. Ade, despite his wounded leg, was with them, and keeping up.

Each rifle had a bayonet attached. The SA80s carried the clip-pointed hollow-handled L3A1 socket bayonet, which fitted over the rifle muzzle. The AK47s, used by the ANA soldiers, took the spear-pointed AK-74 bayonet. Both were deadly.

All Liam could hear was the sound of the soldiers around him raging, baying for blood. They'd all done their bayonet training, and it was anger that enabled a bayonet charge to work. They were screaming and yelling and swearing, their voices breaking, burning their throats raw.

Rounds were flying around them, but the fire was sporadic, the Taliban kept down by the rounds Liam and the rest were putting down as they advanced. It wasn't accurate, but that didn't matter. Its purpose was to keep the enemy pinned down until it was too late. And it was working.

The Taliban were only a few metres away now and Liam called down the line, 'This is it, lads! In at them! Let them have it! Come on, you bastards! *Come on!*'

With a roar, he closed the gap and was into the Taliban position. With his rifle up and ready, all he wanted to do now was take everything out on the enemy and hammer into them with all that he had. He was ready for a fight now. Every part of him was wired for going in close and tearing someone apart. He wasn't violent by nature. None of them were. But when faced with this, and with the training they'd all had, a switch was flicked and they were up for it, blood-and-guts style.

A figure stood up in front of Liam, weapon raised. Liam yelled out, kept charging, managed to drop him with his last remaining rounds. Then his weapon was empty. All that he had left now for sure was the bayonet and his sidearm.

Another Taliban fighter popped up from behind some bushes, but Liam was racing into him even as the man's weapon was raised. He didn't have time to switch to his sidearm. That was seconds lost that were better used with what he was doing now.

Liam screamed, went for it, readied himself for the moment when he'd have to drive the bayonet home, but as he drew close, the Taliban fighter faltered. He fired his weapon from the hip, missing badly, then the weapon jammed. And that was all the excuse he needed. Before Liam was on him, the fighter turned tail and ran.

Liam gave chase, screaming and yelling after him still, but the man could seriously shift and was soon gone, dropping his weapon as he went. Turning back, Liam charged back into the fray, only to find to his utter astonishment that it was already finished.

The smoke cleared and the battlefield became visible.

It was over.

Liam looked around, saw bodies next to weapons. All Taliban.

Clint came over, his eyes still wild from the charge.

'Casualties?'

'None,' said Clint. 'No idea how, but we're all still here.'

'What happened?'

'They scarpered,' Clint said. 'We all saw a few, but they bolted when we turned up. We had enough ammo to deal with any that still wanted a scrap, and a few did – the ones clearly wired on drugs or something –

because they just didn't care, pretty much ran at us as we fired. But it's over, mate, job done.'

Ade joined them, sweat and dust running down his face. 'They fucking shat themselves, Scott,' he said. 'You're a nutter, but it worked.'

Liam still had adrenaline racing through him. His hands were shaking. 'No one used their bayonet then?'

Ade and Clint shook their heads.

'No need,' said Clint. 'It was enough seeing us charge them. Either that or Ade's pug-ugly face sent them scarpering.'

A cry from behind Liam had him zip round. Just metres away was a Taliban fighter, weapon raised and pointed at him. Somehow they'd either missed him, or he'd managed to stay hidden.

The world went into slow motion. Liam dropped his rifle, knowing it was empty, went for his sidearm. He saw Clint and Ade raise their own weapons. Then shots rang out before any of them got a shot off, and the man stalled, sagged to his knees, then fell dead.

Liam looked round to see Zaman with his weapon pointing at where the Taliban fighter had been standing.

In the distance, black dots appeared on the horizon: medevac.

22

'Where's Harding?'

Liam, knackered, grubby, and focusing only on getting rehydrated, was with Lieutenant Steers back at the patrol base. He didn't mind admitting to himself that over the past few hours there had been moments when he'd wondered if he'd ever see it again. It wasn't exactly home, but it still felt good to be there and necking a mug of tea.

'Hitched a ride with the medevac,' said the lieutenant. 'I'm not sure Sunter was all that pleased to have the company.'

'What about Miller and Cowell?'

'Miller has a shoulder wound,' said Steers. 'Lost a lot of blood, but stable. He's had worse, trust me. As for Cowell, he's lucky to be alive. His body armour is completely ruined, but it stopped him getting torn apart. All he's suffered is bruises. Some real whoppers too.'

'And the ANA casualties?'

'As you know, one was unfortunately KIA. The other, I have been informed, is already being operated on.'

Liam looked around as the lads all got themselves settled after the patrol. They were muddy, covered in cuts and bruises and dust, and looked more dead than alive, if he was being honest.

'I'm amazed more of us weren't hit,' said Liam. 'It was an ambush. We were royally fucked from the off.'

'Your actions saved the situation, Scott. Be under no illusion that it was anything else, like luck.'

'It was all we had left,' said Liam. 'Ammunition was low, and we couldn't risk the Taliban getting more reinforcements.'

'Air support?'

'Tally were too close,' Liam said. 'They'd closed in so fast that any air assault would've taken us with them.'

Zaman walked past, offered a smile, nothing more.

'He saved my life,' said Liam. 'We'd missed one. Shah took him out before I got slotted.'

For a moment, Liam and the lieutenant stood in silence. Around them, the soldiers did their best to sort themselves out, but they looked like zombies, an army of the undead trying to figure out what they were supposed to be doing.

'Everyone will need to be TRiM-ed,' said Steers. 'I'll

sort a programme out so that everyone's covered. After what you've all just gone through, a chance to have a chinwag about it seems rather necessary.' He thanked Liam again for his actions, and walked off. Liam caught sight of Cowell and headed over to check on him.

'How you feeling?'

'Sore,' said Cowell, and pointed at the bruises on his chest. He was black and blue. 'Harper's checked me over. Did a thorough job too. Best medic I've worked with. You lot are lucky to have her here to sort you out.'

Liam said nothing, didn't need to. But it was nice to hear Cowell's respect for Nicky voiced.

'She's amazed I've not cracked a rib,' continued Cowell. 'Fucking well hurts like I have, though. Can hardly move.'

'Looks like we're going to be out of action for a while,' said Liam. 'We're men down, you can't move. Not exactly a workable patrol.'

'We'll make do,' said the corporal. 'Either more men will be sent out, or we'll be reassigned. But you're right, I can't move. Not a bloody muscle.' He tried to lie down, but couldn't make it, the pain creasing his face. Liam gave him a hand, helping him to lie and rest on his back.

'Thanks,' said Cowell.

'No problem,' said Liam.

'No,' said Cowell, 'I mean about today. You did good out there, Scott.'

Liam didn't know what to say, stayed quiet.

'You showed initiative, leadership, and above all, balls. A bayonet charge? You mad bastard.' Cowell chuckled, but the laugh was cut off with pain.

'I didn't see much option,' said Liam. He started to speak again but Cowell held up a hand to stop him.

'What other option was there?' he said. 'Ammunition was gone, they were closing in, air support wasn't viable, and you couldn't exactly wait around for the quick reaction force. You did what you had to do and came out the other side.' He looked up, stared Liam in the eye. 'I got you wrong, Scott,' he said. 'And I'm big enough to admit it.'

Liam said nothing. There was nothing he could say – it was time to shut up and listen.

'I gave you a lot of shit at first,' the corporal told him. 'Figured you might be a glory-boy, medal-chasing.'

'I'm not—' started Liam, but Cowell cut him off.

'Like I said, I was wrong, Scott,' he said. 'And that was some serious soldiering there.' He paused, then his expression changed; eyes twinkling, he added, 'Gleaming!'

The corporal closed his eyes and Liam – a bit embarrassed – went back to his own bed. Sitting down, the exhaustion hit him with the weight of a Chieftain tank. He'd had some days in his life, but this one had forced him to learn the hard way a little more about just what he was capable of.

Lying back, still too tired to change, he closed his eyes and sleep took over a heartbeat later.

Up in the sangar again, with Neil, Liam stared out across the Afghanistan landscape, though today he found his mind drifting back to home, looking forward to seeing at least a little rain again, hell – even a road busy with traffic.

A few days had passed since the ambush and life in the compound had resumed its usual routine. It didn't matter how exciting and dangerous things got, there was still a job to do.

News had come back that Miller and Ade were on the mend, and both sent their heartfelt apologies for not being able to join in for the rest of the tour. The ANA soldier was making good progress too.

As one of Cowell's fire team, Neil had been close to the corporal when he'd been hit. 'I thought X-Factor was gone,' he said, holding his sunglasses in his hands to check his own reflection, adjust his fringe. 'Took a hell of a pounding. Must be a hard bastard to come back from that.'

'He'll be in agony for weeks,' said Liam. 'The bruises are huge.'

He stared out into the countryside and found himself wishing to be home, not because he hated his job, but because he wanted to see some green. That would be nice, he thought. A few fields, a tree. Out here, all was the colour of sand and dried mud. The plants that survived were hardy. It was not a lush countryside by any means, and sometimes it was hard on the eye.

A head appeared at the top of the steps up into the sangar. It was Cowell, and for once he didn't look like he was there to chew them up over something. He made his way slowly up to join Liam and Neil.

'Quiet, is it?'

Liam nodded. 'Nothing,' he said. 'I think they've bugged out completely after what happened. No surprise really – they took a beating.'

'Can't blame them, can you?' Cowell replied. 'A bunch of mad bastards charge you with spears, you're bound to think twice about coming back to have a go.'

Liam smiled and Neil laughed.

'Can't see it becoming generally accepted practice, though,' said Neil. 'You know, every patrol doing a bayonet charge, that kind of thing. Fun though it is, clearly.'

Cowell moved forward between Neil and Liam. It

was clear that he was still in pain. 'Quite a country really, isn't it?' he said. 'Not sure I'd book a two-week break here, though, know what I mean?'

'I've seen worse places,' said Neil. 'Honestly, if you ever get the chance to visit my home town, Swindon – don't. It's a shit hole.'

'Good advice,' said Liam, then turned to Cowell. 'So why did you join up?' he asked. 'Carter's here because apparently the army begged him to join, right?'

'Too right,' said Neil.

With a laugh, Cowell said, 'It was all I ever wanted to do. Never thought of anything else.'

'Really?' asked Liam.

'Totally,' said Cowell. 'As a kid, it was all I thought about, joining up. Couldn't wait to hit sixteen and get on with it. And that's what I did.'

'Any plans to leave, then?'

'Not yet,' said Cowell. 'Not sure what I'd do if I—'

By the time Liam heard the distant rifle crack, it was already too late, cutting the corporal off mid-sentence. The round, with hellish accuracy, smashed into Cowell's face, just below his right eye, shattering his cheekbone. It then continued through his head, taking a large part of it with it as it exited, finally coming to a stop in the sandbags at the back of the sangar.

Cowell, dead on his feet, dropped like liquid. There

was no grace about it, no muscles to stop him smashing into the ground in one big pile of violent death.

Liam and Neil, momentarily stunned by what had happened, stared at Cowell. Not five seconds ago he'd been speaking. Now he was gone.

They were on their weapons, scanning the ground immediately, Neil with his sniper rifle, Liam with the Sharpshooter.

'Eleven o'clock,' said Liam. 'Possible contact.'

Neil swung his weapon. 'Confirmed. I have two.'

'One dicker, one shooter,' said Liam. 'Out at four-twenty metres. You take the dicker. On your mark.'

Liam breathed in, then relaxed, finger on the trigger. He squeezed, just enough, waiting for Neil.

'Now.'

Liam and Neil both squeezed their triggers. The rifles fired almost simultaneously.

Liam saw the dicker kicked up into the air as Neil's round took him in the chest. His own round crashed into the skull of the shooter.

They both chambered another round.

'Kill confirmed,' said Neil.

'Confirmed,' said Liam.

Silence.

Neither Liam nor Neil moved. At their feet, Cowell's body lay still.

'Carter? Scott? What the hell was that? What are you shooting at?'

It was Steers, but when he saw Cowell he stopped dead.

'Oh, fuck.'

'Sniper,' said Liam. 'And a dicker.'

'Where?'

Neil motioned with a sideways nod of his head. 'Just over four hundred metres out, sir,' he said. 'And they're not going anywhere.'

'Imminent threat to life, sir,' said Liam. 'We had to take the shot.'

The lieutenant, Liam noticed, looked grey, all colour drained from his face. 'I'll get Nicky,' he said, 'and radio this in.' Then he was gone.

'So the whole multiple is being pulled back?'

Liam was with Clint and Nicky, each of them nursing a mug of tea.

'Yes,' said Liam, answering Clint's question. 'We're four men down. So we're back to Bastion. After that, I haven't a clue.'

With half of their tour still to do, they were all uncertain about what would happen next.

'We'll probably all be just reassigned,' said Nicky. 'Join another multiple to see out the rest of the tour.'

'Any plans after that?' Liam asked.

Nicky put her mug down. 'I'm an army brat,' she said. 'This is all I know.'

'Cowboy?'

'I've got my family and my business back home,' he said. 'And I'm TA, so it's different to you lot. I do this as extra.'

'Which strikes me as completely mental,' said Liam.

Clint fired the question back at Liam. 'What about you? You're the newest to this. Any thoughts?'

'I want to go career,' said Liam, the words out of his mouth before he'd really even had a chance to think about what he was saying.

'You need to try and grow a beard first, surely,' said Clint, 'before you go making any adult decisions.'

As their laughter died, another figure joined them. It was Zaman. Liam asked him to sit, but immediately knew something was bothering him.

'What's up?'

'I have found out how it all happened,' said Zaman. 'The ambush.'

Liam, Clint and Nicky leaned in.

'I will tell the lieutenant, but you are my friend and I wanted to tell you first, Scott. And you saved everyone's lives by your brave actions. It seems only fair.'

Liam simply allowed Zaman to keep speaking.

'The soldier who shot Cowell, like me, he also has a brother in the Taliban. But unlike me, where I do not share their beliefs, he did. It was he who set it up.'

'How?' asked Clint.

'He was able to get information out to his brother,' said Zaman. 'There are always ways, and no amount of checking can ever stop it.'

'So he told them where we would be?'

Zaman nodded. 'The weapons cache was simply to give the Taliban a chance to observe you, watch you react to a small attack from a sniper, count your numbers. The second was to capture and kill.'

'Capture?' said Nicky.

Zaman said, 'Yes. It was all planned. They would have paraded the largest taking of soldier prisoners on the TV screens. It would have been a major blow to everything you and the ANA are doing to help our country know peace.'

'And if they'd taken prisoners?' asked Nicky. 'Then what?'

'It would have been as I'm sure you already know,' said Zaman. He stood up. 'I will say goodbye now, Scott,' he said. 'It has been good to work with you.'

Liam stood up. He'd learned a lot from Zaman, not just about Afghanistan, but about himself.

'And with you, Shah. Thank you. What will you do now?'

'Continue my work,' Zaman replied. 'And look forward to peace. To see my brother again, that would also be good, but . . .' His voice faded and Liam spotted a look of sorrow in his eyes.

'I hope that happens,' said Liam. 'I really do, Shah.'

'*Mersi mamoon*,' said Zaman. 'Thank you, Scott. And you will continue with your Dari, yes?'

'*Man say mikonam ke yad begiram*,' said Liam: 'Yes, I will try.'

Zaman smiled. '*Bezoodi shoma ra behinam*, Liam,' he said, bowing a little, then left.

'What did he say?' asked Nicky.

'He said see you soon,' said Liam.

'Doubt there's much chance of that,' she said.

'You never know,' said Liam, watching as Zaman walked away. 'You just never know.'

Real coffee was one thing, but iced coffee, now that was something else. Liam, now back at Camp Bastion, having arrived a day earlier in the back of a Chinook, enjoyed every single drop as he drained his cup. Then, without hesitation, he got up from his table and went to order another. Caffeine and ice, he thought – what could be better?

He sat down again with his second coffee and took his first sip. God, he'd missed this!

'Excuse me?'

Liam looked up over his drink to see three soldiers.

'These seats taken?'

'No,' said Liam. 'Help yourself.'

The soldiers nodded a thank you and took their seats. Liam noticed then from the way they looked that they must have only just arrived. They looked too clean and too keen to be anything else.

'Tour just started?' he asked.

'Yes,' said one of the soldiers. 'I'm guessing that you've been out here a while.'

'Second tour,' said Liam. 'Things got a bit noisy, if you know what I mean, so I'm back here waiting to be redeployed.'

'What happened?'

Liam told them, but kept the details brief. When he'd finished, he noticed a look of acknowledgement in the soldiers' faces.

'What?' he asked.

'So you were in the bayonet charge,' said one of the soldiers. 'We heard about that.'

'Really?'

'Word gets round fast, clearly,' said another of the soldiers. 'Took some serious balls, that, though.'

'Didn't have any choice,' said Liam, playing it down. 'Anyone would've done the same.'

The look the soldiers gave him made it very clear they didn't quite agree.

'So what are you lot in?' Liam asked, changing the subject.

'Recce Platoon,' said the soldier who'd first spoken to him.

Liam remembered Cowell mentioning them in the same breath as the SAS and Pathfinders. He didn't know much about what they did, but something about these lads in front of him piqued his interest.

'Sneaky beaky boys, then, right?' said Liam.

The soldiers laughed. 'I guess,' one of them said.

'So how do I join?'

'Why, are you interested?'

Liam stared into his coffee, then looked around. The army was his home now. Something about it had got a hold of him and wouldn't let go. He was himself here. But not only that, he was growing too, becoming someone that a couple of years ago he could never have even imagined. He didn't just want to do it for a while, he wanted to make a proper go of it – of that he was sure.

Liam drained his coffee.

'Yes,' he said. 'I am.'

Author's Note

The Afghanistan War

Afghanistan is a country where there have been a number of conflicts over the years. Many regions are controlled by tribal warlords, who have a lot of experience of fighting within the harsh landscape. The Taliban – mostly made up of tribal leaders – is a political movement with strong Islamist fundamental beliefs who took power in Afghanistan from 1996 to 2001.

The current war there began in 2001, when Afghanistan gave support to the terrorist organization Al-Qaeda and its leader, Osama bin Laden, who was held responsible for the terrorist attack in the United States on New York's Twin Towers. The United States, supported by its allies – including the United Kingdom – and the anti-Taliban Northern Alliance forces launched an offensive and drove the Taliban out of power.

But the Taliban continued to fight for power, and UK troops were among those sent to the country as NATO-led foreign peacekeepers, to try and establish peace in the region. A permanent Afghan government was elected in 2004, but peace was still a long way off for the Afghani population.

After Bin Laden was killed in Pakistan in 2011, leaders of the NATO countries agreed a timetable to withdraw from Afghanistan. At the time of writing this book – 2013 – UK troops are still in the country, but now, like Liam, working primarily in a support and training role with the Afghan National Army.

The exit date for all NATO combat troops is planned for the end of 2014.

Andy McNab, October 2013

ACKNOWLEDGEMENTS

FROM DIRECTORATE MEDIA AND COMMUNICATIONS, MINISTRY OF DEFENCE:

Lt Col Crispin Lockhart

FROM ARMY MEDIA AND COMMUNICATIONS:

Mr Charles Heath-Saunders

FROM QUEEN'S ROYAL LANCERS:

Captain John Madocks Wright